"We hardly know each other, Lucy.

"I'm not sure why you're so confident about who I am and what I do or don't think of you. But here... I'll prove to you that you're wrong."

He took two steps forward, closing the gap between them. Lucy stiffened as he got closer, but she held her ground.

"What are you doing?" She looked up at him with big brown eyes that were full of uncertainty.

She thought she could just call his bluff and he'd back down. No way. He was going all in and winning the hand even with losing cards.

Oliver eased forward until they were almost touching. He dipped his head down to her and cupped her face in his hands. Tilting her mouth up to him, he pressed his lips against hers. He wanted this kiss to be gentle, sweet and meaningless, so he could prove his point and move on with his night. He'd kissed a lot of women in his time. This would be like any other.

Or so he thought.

* * *

Rags to Riches Baby is part of the Millionaires of Manhattan series from Andrea Laurence.

Dear Reader,

The idea for this book came straight from the headlines. A few years back, I read an article about a reclusive Manhattan heiress who left her massive fortune to her nurse. I knew it would be the perfect premise for the right character and Lucy was the one. Putting myself in her shoes—imagining what it would be like to wake up a millionaire—was harder than expected, especially since Lucy refused to cooperate. Growing up poor like I did, she was a little jaded and refused to believe something like this could happen to a girl like her. Nor did she think that a man like Oliver would come into her life either! I really got to shake things up for Lucy, thrusting her into a world she never dreamed of, and taking readers along for the ride.

If you enjoy Lucy and Oliver's story, tell me by visiting my website at www.andrealaurence.com, liking my fan page on Facebook or following me on Twitter.

Enjoy,

Andrea

ANDREA LAURENCE

RAGS TO RICHES BABY

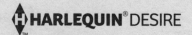

Recycling programs
for this product may
not exist in your area.

ISBN-13: 978-1-335-97132-6

Rags to Riches Baby

Copyright © 2018 by Andrea Laurence

Printed in U.S.A.

www.Harlequin.com

Andrea Laurence is an award-winning author of contemporary romances filled with seduction and sass. She has been a lover of reading and writing stories since she was young. A dedicated West Coast girl transplanted into the Deep South, she is thrilled to share her special blend of sensuality and dry, sarcastic humor with readers.

Books by Andrea Laurence

Harlequin Desire

Brides and Belles

Snowed In with Her Ex
Thirty Days to Win His Wife
One Week with the Best Man
A White Wedding Christmas

Millionaires of Manhattan

What Lies Beneath
More Than He Expected
His Lover's Little Secret
The CEO's Unexpected Child
Little Secrets: Secretly Pregnant
Rags to Riches Baby

Hawaiian Nights

The Pregnancy Proposition
The Baby Proposal

Visit her Author Profile page at Harlequin.com, or andrealaurence.com, for more titles.

To Dr. Shelley—

Thanks for dusting off your MoMA catalog and helping me navigate the modern art references for this book. I never would've found those pieces on my own. I also never expected to find myself watching a YouTube video of naked women in blue paint pressing against a canvas while a string quartet played. Your suggestions were perfect for the book! Thank you!

One

"And to Lucy Campbell, my assistant and companion, I bequeath the remainder of my estate, including the balances of my accounts and financial holdings and the whole of my personal effects, which entails my art collection and my apartment on Fifth Avenue."

When the attorney stopped reading the will of Alice Drake aloud, the room was suddenly so quiet Lucy wondered if the rest of the Drake family had dropped dead as well at the unexpected news. She kept waiting for the lawyer to crack a smile and tell the crowd of people around the conference room table that he was just kidding. It seemed highly inappropriate to do to a grieving family, though.

Surely, he had to be kidding. Lucy was no real estate expert, but Alice's apartment alone had to be worth over twenty million dollars. It overlooked the Metropolitan Museum of Art. It had four bedrooms and a gallery with a dozen important works, including an original Monet, hanging in it. Lucy couldn't afford the monthly association fees for the co-op, much less own an apartment like that in Manhattan.

"Are you serious?" a sharp voice cut through the silence at last.

Finally, someone was asking the question that was on the tip of her own tongue. Lucy turned toward the voice and realized it was her best friend Harper Drake's brother, Oliver. Harper had helped Lucy get this job working for her great-aunt, but she'd never met Harper's brother before today. Which was odd, considering she'd cared for their aunt for over five years.

It was a shame. He was one of the most handsome men she'd ever seen in real life and since he was across the conference table from her, she had a great view. Harper was a pretty woman, but the same aristocratic features on Oliver were striking in a different way. They both had the same wavy brown hair, sharp cheekbones and pointed chins, but he had the blue-gray eyes and permanently furrowed brow of their father. His lips were thinner than Harper's, but she wasn't sure if they were always like that or if they were just pressed together in irritation at the moment.

His gaze flicked over Lucy, and she felt an unexpected surge of desire run down her spine. The tingle it left in its wake made a flush rise to her cheeks and she squirmed uncomfortably in her seat. She didn't know if it was the surprising news or his heavy appraisal of her, but it was suddenly warm in the small conference room. Lucy reached for the button at the collar of her blouse and undid it as quickly as she could, drawing in a deep breath.

Unfortunately, that breath was scented with the sharp cologne of the man across from her. It teased at her nose, making the heat in her belly worsen.

It was painfully apparent that she'd spent far too many years in the company of a ninety-plus-year-old woman. One handsome man looked at her, and she got all flustered. Lucy needed to pull herself together. This was not the time to get distracted, especially when the man in question was anything but an ally. She closed her eyes for a moment and was relieved to find when she'd reopened them that Oliver had returned his focus to the attorney.

Yes, Lucy definitely would've remembered if he'd stopped by to visit. Actually, she hadn't met any of these people before Alice died and they all started showing up to the apartment. She recognized a few of them from pictures on the mantel, but they hadn't visited Alice when she was alive that Lucy was aware of. And Alice certainly hadn't gone to see them. She was ninety-three when she died and still an eccentric free spirit despite confining herself to her apartment for decades. Lucy had been drawn to her radically different beat, but not everyone would be. She'd thought perhaps Alice's family just didn't "get" her.

Judging by the stunned and angry looks on their faces, they all seemed to think they were much closer to Aunt Alice than they truly were.

"Really, Phillip. Is this some sort of a joke?" This time it was Thomas Drake, Harper and Oliver's father and Alice's nephew, who spoke. He was an older version of Oliver, with gray streaks in his hair and a distinguished-looking beard. It didn't hide his frown, however.

Phillip Glass, Alice's attorney and executor of her estate, shook his head with a grim expression on his face. He didn't look like the joking kind. "I'm sorry, but I'm very serious. I discussed this with Alice at length when she decided to make the change to her will earlier this year. I had hoped she spoke with all of you about her wishes, but apparently, that is not the case. All of you were to receive a monetary gift of fifty thousand dollars each, but she was very clear that everything else was to go to Lucy."

"She must've been suffering from dementia,"

a sour-looking woman Lucy didn't recognize said from the far end of the table.

"She was not!" Lucy retorted, suddenly feeling defensive where Alice was concerned. She'd had a bad heart and a fondness for good wines and cheeses, but she wasn't at all impaired mentally. Actually, for her age, she was in amazing shape up until her death.

"Of course *you* would say that!" the woman retorted with a red flush to her face. "She was obviously losing her senses when she made these changes."

"And how would you know?" Lucy snapped. "Not a one of you set foot in her apartment for the five years I've cared for her. You have no idea how she was doing. You only came sniffing around when it was time to claim your part of her estate."

The older woman clutched her pearls, apparently aghast that Lucy would speak to her that way. Lucy didn't care. She wouldn't have these people besmirching Alice after her death when they didn't know anything about how wonderful she was.

Harper reached out and gripped Lucy's forearm. "It's okay, Lucy. They're just surprised and upset at the news. They'll get over it."

"I will not get over it!" the woman continued. "I can't believe you're taking the help's side in this, Harper. She's basically stealing your inheritance right out from under you!"

"The *help*?" Harper's voice shot up an octave before Lucy could respond. The time for calm had instantly passed. "Wanda, you need to apologize right now. I will not have you speaking about my friend that way. Aunt Alice obviously felt Lucy was more than just an employee as well, so you should treat her with the same respect."

Lucy started to shut down as Alice's relatives fought amongst themselves. The last few days of her life had been hard. Finding Alice's body, dealing with the funeral and having her life upended all at once had been too much on its own. That was the risk of being a live-in employee. Losing her client meant losing her friend, her job and her home.

And now she found herself in the middle of the Drake family money battle. Lucy wasn't one for conflict to begin with, and this was the last thing she'd anticipated when she'd been asked to come today. At best, she thought perhaps Alice had left her a little money as a severance package until she could find a new job and a place to live. She had no real idea how much Alice was worth, but from the reactions of the family, she'd been left more than a little money. Like millions.

For a girl who'd grown up poor and gone to college on a scholarship and a prayer, it was all too much to take in at once. Especially when Oliver's steely blue eyes returned to watching her from across the table. He seemed to look right through her skin and into her soul. She felt the prickle of goose bumps rise across her flesh at the thought of being so exposed to him, but she immediately tried to shelve the sense of self-awareness he brought out in her. If he was studying her, it was only to seek out a weakness to exploit or an angle to work. He might be Harper's brother, but he was obviously no friend to Lucy.

The spell was finally broken as he casually turned away to look at his sister. "I know she's your friend, Harper, but you have to admit there's something fishy about this whole thing." Oliver's rich baritone voice drew Lucy back into the conversation.

"Fishy, how?" Lucy asked.

"I wouldn't blame you for influencing her to leave you something. You're alone with her day after day. It would be easy to drop hints and convince her it was her idea to leave you everything." Oliver's blue eyes narrowed at her again, nearly pinning Lucy to the back of her leather chair with his casual accusation.

"Are you serious?" She repeated his earlier question. "I had no idea about any of this. We never discussed her will or her money. Not once in five years. I didn't even know why Phillip called me in here today. I'm just as surprised as you are."

"I highly doubt that," Wanda muttered.

"Please, folks," Phillip interjected. "I realize this

is a shock to all of you. I wish I could say something to make things better, but the bottom line is that this is what Alice wanted. Feel free to retain a lawyer if you're interested in challenging the will in court, but as it stands, Lucy gets everything."

Wanda pushed up from her seat and slung her Hermès purse dramatically over her arm. "You bet I'm calling my attorney," she said as she headed for the door. "What a waste of a fortune!"

The rest of the family shuffled out behind her until it was only Harper, Lucy and Phillip sitting at the table.

"I'm sorry about all that, Lucy," the attorney said. "Alice should've prepared the family so this wasn't such a shock to them. She probably avoided it because they'd have pressured her to change it back. With this crowd, I'd anticipate a fight. That means you won't be able to sell the apartment and most of the accounts will likely be frozen until it's resolved in court. Alice put a stipulation into the will that authorizes me to maintain all the expenses for the apartment and continue paying you and the housekeeper in the event the will is contested, so you won't have to worry about any of that. I'll do my best to get some cash available for you before her family files, but don't go spending a bunch of it right away."

Lucy couldn't imagine that was possible. She'd made a lot of wealthy friends while at Yale, but she'd always been the thrifty one in the group by necessity. Thankfully, her sorority sisters Violet, Emma and Harper had never treated her any differently.

Having her penniless circumstances change so suddenly seemed impossible. Nearly every dime she made from working for Alice went into savings for her to finish school. She wouldn't even know what she'd do with money in her accounts that wasn't earmarked for something else.

"Wanda is full of hot air," Harper said. "She'll complain but she won't lay out a penny of her own money to contest the will. More than likely, they'll all sit back and let Oliver handle it."

Lucy frowned. "Your brother seemed really angry. Is he going to take it out on you?"

Harper snorted. "No. He knows better. Oliver will leave the battle to the courtroom. But don't be surprised if he shows up at the apartment ready to give you the third degree. He's a seasoned businessman, so he'll be on the hunt for any loophole he can exploit."

Lucy's first thought was that she wouldn't mind Harper's brother visiting, but his handsome face wouldn't make up for his ill intentions. He intended to overturn Alice's wishes and was probably going to be successful. Lucy didn't have the means to fight him. She could blow every penny she'd saved on attorneys and still wouldn't have enough to beat a man with his means. It was a waste of money anyway. Things like this just didn't happen to women like her. The rich got richer, after all.

That did beg the question she was afraid to ask while the others were still around. "Phillip, Alice and I never really discussed her finances. How much money are we talking about here?"

Phillip flipped through a few papers and swallowed hard. "Well, it looks like between the apartment, her investments, cash accounts and personal property, you're set to inherit about five hundred million dollars, Lucy."

Lucy frowned and leaned toward the attorney in confusion. "I—I'm sorry, I think I heard you wrong, Phillip. Could you repeat that?"

Harper took Lucy's hand and squeezed it tight. "You heard him correctly, Lucy. Aunt Alice was worth half a billion dollars and she's left most of it to you. I know it's hard for you to believe, but congratulations. It couldn't happen to a better person."

Lucy's breath caught in her throat, the words stolen from her lips. That wasn't possible. It just wasn't possible. It was like her numbers were just called in the lotto. The odds were stacked against a woman like her—someone who came from nothing and was expected to achieve even less. Half a *billion*? No wonder Alice's family was upset.

The help had just become a multimillionaire.

So that was the infamous Lucy Campbell.

Oliver had heard plenty about her over the years

from his sister and in emails from his aunt. For some reason, he'd expected her to be more attractive. Instead, her hair was a dark, mousy shade of dishwater blond, her nails were in need of a manicure and her eyes were too big for her face. He was pretty sure she was wearing a hand-me-down suit of Harper's.

All in all, she seemed incredibly ordinary for someone with her reputation. Aunt Alice was notoriously difficult to impress and she'd written at length about her fondness for Lucy. He'd almost been intrigued enough to pay a visit and learn more about her. Maybe then he wouldn't have been as disappointed.

She had freckles. Actual *freckles*. He'd never known anyone with freckles before. He'd only remained calm in the lawyer's office by trying to count the sprinkle of them across her nose and cheeks. He wondered how many more there were. Were they only on her face, or did they continue across her shoulders and chest?

He'd lost count at thirty-two.

After that, he'd decided to focus on the conversation. He'd found himself responding to her in a way he hadn't anticipated when he first laid eyes on her. The harder he looked, the more he saw. But then she turned her gaze back on him and he found the reciprocal scrutiny uncomfortable. Those large, doe eyes seemed so innocent and looked at him with a pleading expression he didn't care for. It made him feel things that would muddy the situation.

Instead, Oliver decided he was paying far too much attention to her and she didn't deserve it. She was a sneaky, greedy liar just like his stepmother and he had no doubt of it. Harper didn't see it and maybe Alice didn't either, but Oliver had his eyes wide open. Just like when his father had fallen for Candace with her pouty lips and fake breasts, Oliver could see through the pretty facade.

Okay, so maybe Lucy was pretty. But that was it. Just pretty. Nothing spectacular. Certainly nothing like the elegant, graceful women that usually hung on his arm at society events around Manhattan. She was more like the cute barista at the corner coffee shop that he tipped extra just because she always remembered he liked extra foam.

Yeah, that. Lucy was pretty like that.

He couldn't imagine her rubbing elbows with the wealthy and esteemed elite of New York City. There was new money, and then there was the kind of person who never should've had it. Like a lottery winner. That was a fluke of luck and mathematics, but it didn't change who the person really was or where they belonged. He had a hard time thinking Manhattan high society would accept Lucy even with millions at her disposal.

His stepmother, Candace, had been different. She was young and beautiful, graceful with a dancer's build. She could hold her own with the rich crowd as though she'd always belonged there. Her smile lit up the room and despite the fact that she was more than twenty years younger, Oliver's father had been drawn to her like a fly to honey.

Oliver looked up and noticed his driver had arrived back at his offices. It was bad enough he had to leave in the middle of the day to deal with his aunt's estate. Returning with fifty thousand in his pocket was hardly worth the time he'd lost.

"Thank you, Harrison." Oliver got out of the black sedan and stepped onto the curb outside of Orion headquarters. He looked at the brass plaque on the wall declaring the name of the company his father had started in the eighties. Tom Drake had been at the forefront of the home computer boom. By the turn of the new millennium, one out of every five home computers purchased was an Orion.

Then Candace happened and it all fell apart.

Oliver pushed through the revolving doors and headed to his private elevator in the far corner of the marble-and-brass-filled lobby. Orion's corporate offices occupied the three top floors of the forty-floor high-rise he'd purchased six years earlier. As he slipped his badge into the slot, it started rocketing him past the other thirty-nine floors to take him directly to the area outside the Orion executive offices.

Production and shipping took place in a facility about fifteen miles away in New Jersey. There, the latest and greatest laptops, tablets and smartphones produced by his company were assembled and shipped to stores around the country.

Everyone had told Oliver that producing their products in the US instead of Asia or Mexico was crazy. That they'd improve their stock prices by going overseas and increase their profit margins. They said he should move their call centers to India like his competitors.

He hadn't listened to any of them, and thankfully, he'd had a board that backed his crazy ideas. It was succeed or go home by the time his father handed over the reins of the company. He'd rebuilt his father's business through ingenuity, hard work and more than a little luck.

When the elevator doors opened, Oliver made his way to the corner suite he took over six years ago. That was when Candace disappeared and his father decided to retire from Orion to care for their two-year-old son she'd left behind.

Oliver hated to see his father's heart broken, and he didn't dare say that he'd told him so the minute Candace showed up. But Oliver had known what she was about from the beginning.

Lucy was obviously made from the same cloth, although instead of romancing an older widower, she'd befriended an elderly shut-in without any direct heirs.

His aunt Alice had always been different and he'd appreciated that about her, even as a child. After she decided to lock herself away in her fancy apartment, Oliver gifted her with a state-of-the-art laptop and set her up with an email address so they could stay in touch. He'd opted to respect her need to be alone.

Now he regretted it. He'd let his sister's endorsement of Lucy cloud his judgment. Maybe if he'd stopped by, maybe if he'd seen Lucy and Alice interact, he could've stopped this before it went too far.

Oliver threw open the door to his office in irritation, startling his assistant.

"Are you okay, Mr. Drake?" Monica asked with wide eyes.

Oliver frowned. He didn't need to lose his cool at work. Letting emotions affect him would be his father's mistake, and look what that had done. "I am. I'm sorry, Monica."

"I'm sorry about your aunt. I saw an article about her in the paper that said she'd locked herself in her apartment for almost twenty years. Was that true?"

Oliver sighed. His aunt had drawn plenty of interest alive and dead. "No. Only seventeen years," he said with a smile.

Monica seemed stunned by the very idea. "I can't imagine not leaving my apartment for that long."

"Well," Oliver pointed out, "she had a very nice apartment. She wasn't exactly suffering there."

"Will you inherit her place? I know you two were

close and the article said she didn't have any children."

The possibility had been out there until this afternoon when everything changed. Aunt Alice had never married or had children of her own. A lot of people assumed that he and Harper would be the ones to inherit the bulk of her estate. Oliver didn't need his aunt's money or her apartment; it wasn't really his style. But he resented a woman wiggling her way into the family and stealing it out from under them.

Especially a woman with wide eyes and irritatingly fascinating freckles that had haunted his thoughts for the last hour.

"I doubt it, but you never know. Hold my calls, will you, Monica?"

She nodded as he slipped into his office and shut the door. He was in no mood to talk to anyone. He'd cleared his calendar for the afternoon, figuring he would be in discussions with his family about Alice's estate for some time. Instead, everyone had rushed out in a panic and he'd followed them.

It was best that he left when he did. The longer he found himself in the company of the alluring Miss Campbell, the more intrigued he became. It was ridiculous, really. She was the kind of woman he wouldn't give a second glance to on the street. But seated across from him at that conference room table, looking at him like her fate was in his hands…

he needed some breathing room before he did something stupid.

He pulled his phone out of his pocket and glanced at the screen before tossing it onto his desk. Harper had called him twice in the last half hour, but he'd turned the ringer off. His sister was likely on a mission to convince him to let the whole issue with the will drop. They'd have to agree to disagree where Lucy and her inheritance was concerned.

Oliver settled into his executive chair with a shake of his head and turned to look out the wall of windows to his view of the city. His office faced the west on one side and north on the other. In an hour or so, he'd have a great view of the sun setting over the Hudson. He rarely looked at it. His face was always buried in spreadsheets or he was doodling madly on the marker board. Something always needed his attention and he liked it that way. If he was busy, that meant the company was successful.

Free time…he didn't have much of it, and when he did, he hardly knew what to do with it. He kept a garden, but that was just a stress reliever. He dated from time to time, usually at Harper's prodding, but never anything very serious.

He couldn't help but see shades of Candace in every woman that gave a coy smile and batted her thick lashes at him. He knew that wasn't the right attitude to have—there were plenty of women with money of their own who were interested in him for more than just his fortune and prestige. He just wasn't certain how to tell them apart.

One thing he did notice today was that Lucy Campbell neither smiled or batted her lashes at him. At first, her big brown eyes had looked him over with a touch of disgust wrinkling her pert, freckled nose. A woman had never grazed over him with her eyes the way she had. It was almost as though he smelled like something other than the expensive cologne he'd splashed on that morning.

He'd been amused by her reaction to him initially. At least until they started reading the will. Once he realized who she was and what she'd done, it wasn't funny any longer.

Harper believed one hundred percent in Lucy's innocence. They'd been friends since college. She probably knew Lucy better than anyone else and normally, he would take his sister's opinion as gospel. But was she too close? Harper could be blinded to the truth by her friendship, just as their father had been blinded to the truth by his love for Candace. In both instances, hundreds of millions were at stake.

Even the most honest, honorable person could be tempted to get a tiny piece of that pie. Alice had been ninety-three. Perhaps Lucy looked at her with those big, sad eyes and told Alice a sob story about needing the money. Perhaps she'd charmed his aunt into thinking of her as the child she never had.

Maybe Lucy only expected a couple million and her scheme worked out even better than she planned.

Either way, it didn't matter how it came about. The bottom line was that Lucy had manipulated his aunt and he wasn't going to sit by and let her profit from it. This was a half-billion-dollar estate—they weren't quibbling over their grandmother's Chippendale dresser or Wedgwood China. He couldn't—wouldn't—let this go without a fight. His aunt deserved that much.

With a sigh, he reached for his phone and dialed his attorney. Freckles be damned, Lucy Campbell and her charms would be no match for Oliver and his team of bloodthirsty lawyers.

Two

Lucy awoke the next morning with the same odd sense of pressure on her chest. It had been like that since the day she'd discovered Alice had died in her sleep and her world had turned upside down. Discovering she could potentially be a millionaire and Alice's entire family hated her had done little to ease that pressure. It may actually be worse since they met with Phillip.

Someone would undoubtedly contest the will, which would put Alice's estate in limbo until it was resolved. When she asked Phillip how long that would take, he said it could be weeks to months. The family's attorneys would search for any way they could to nullify the latest will. That meant dragging their "dear aunt's" reputation through the mud along with Lucy's. Either Alice wasn't in her right mind—and many would argue she never had been—or Lucy had manipulated her.

It made Lucy wonder if she could decline the inheritance. Was that an option? While the idea of all that money and stuff seemed nice, she didn't want to be ripped to shreds to get it. She hadn't manipulated Alice, and Alice hadn't been crazy. She'd obviously just decided that her family either didn't deserve or need the money. Since she never discussed it with anyone but Phillip and hadn't been forthcoming about her reasoning even to him, they would never know.

Alice had been quirky that way. She never left her apartment, but she had plenty of stories from her youth about how she enjoyed going against the flow, especially where her family was involved. If it was possible for her to listen in on her will reading from heaven, Lucy was pretty sure she was cracking up. Alice would've found the look on Wanda's face in particular to be priceless.

While the decision was being made, Lucy found herself at a loss. What, exactly, was she supposed to be doing with her time? Her client was dead, but she was still receiving her salary, room and board. After the funeral, Lucy had started putting together plans to pick up her life where she'd been forced to drop it. She had a year left in her art history program at Yale. Her scholarship hadn't covered all four years and without it, there was no way she had been able to continue.

Working and living with Alice had allowed her to save almost all of her salary and she had a tidy little nest egg now that she could use to move back to Connecticut and finish school. Then, hopefully, she could use the connections she'd established the last few years in the art world to land a job at a prestigious museum.

Alice and Lucy had bonded over art. Honestly, Lucy'd had no experience as a home health nurse or caregiver of any kind, but that wasn't really what Alice needed. She needed a companion, a helper around the apartment. She also needed someone who would go out into the world for her. Part of that had included attending gallery openings and art auctions in Alice's place. Lucy had met quite a few people there and with Alice Drake's reputation behind her, hopefully those connections would carry forward once she entered the art community herself.

Today, Lucy found herself sitting in the library staring at the computer screen and her readmission forms for Yale, but she couldn't focus on them. Her gaze kept drifting around the apartment to all the things she'd never imagined would be hers. Certainly not the apartment itself, with its prewar moldings, handcrafted built-ins and polished, inlaid hardwood floors. Not the gallery of art pieces that looked like a wing of the Met or MoMA. It was all lovely, but nothing she would ever need to worry about personally.

Except now, she had to worry about it all, including the college forms. It was September. If this court hearing dragged through the fall, it would mess with her returning to school for the spring semester. Phillip had recommended she not move out, even if she didn't want to keep the apartment. He was worried members of the family would squat in it and make it difficult for her to take ownership or sell it even if the judge ruled in her favor. That meant the pile of boxes in the corner she'd started to fill up would stay put for now and Yale in January might not happen.

All because Alice decided Lucy should be a millionaire and everyone else disagreed.

The sound of the doorbell echoed through the apartment, distracting Lucy from her worries. She saved her work and shut the laptop before heading out to the front door. Whoever was here must be on the visitor list or the doorman wouldn't have let them up. She hoped it was Harper, but one glance out the peephole dashed those hopes.

It was Oliver Drake.

Lucy smoothed her hands over her hair and opened the door to greet her guest. He was wearing one of a hundred suits he likely owned, this one being navy instead of the black he'd worn to the lawyer's office the day before. Navy looked better on him. It brought out the blue in his eyes and for some reason, highlighted the gold strands in his brown, wavy hair.

She tore her gaze away from her inspection and instead focused on his mildly sour expression. Not a pleasure visit, she could tell, so she decided to set the tone before he could. "Oliver, so glad to see you were able to find the place. Do come in."

She took a step back and Oliver entered the apartment with his gaze never leaving hers. "I have been here before, you know. Dozens of times."

"But so much has changed since the nineties. Please, feel free to take a look around and reacquaint yourself with the apartment." Lucy closed the door and when she turned around, found that Oliver was still standing in the same spot, studying her.

"You know, I can't tell if you're always this cheeky or if you're doing it because you've got something to hide. Are you nervous, Lucy?" His voice was low and even, seemingly unbothered by her cutting quips.

Lucy crossed her arms over her chest and took a step back from him, as though doing so would somehow shield her from the blue eyes that threatened to see too much. "I don't have anything to be nervous about."

He took two slow strides toward her, moving

into her personal space and forcing her back until the doorknob pressed into her spine. He was over six foot, lurking over her and making Lucy feel extremely petite at her five-foot-four-inch height. He leaned down close, studying her face with such intensity she couldn't breathe.

Oliver paused at her lips for a moment, sending confusing signals to Lucy's brain. She didn't think Harper's arrogant older brother would kiss her, but stranger things had already happened this week. Instead, his gaze shifted to her eyes, pinning her against the door of the apartment without even touching her. By this point, Lucy's heart was pounding so loudly in her ears, it was nearly deafening her during his silent appraisal.

"We'll see about that," he said at last.

When he finally took a step back, Lucy felt like she could breathe again. There was something intense about Oliver that made her uncomfortable, especially when he looked at her that way.

As though nothing had just happened between them, Oliver stuffed his hands into his pockets and started strolling casually through the gallery and into the great room. Lucy followed him with a frown lining her face. She didn't understand what he wanted. Was this just some psychological game he was playing with her? Was he looking to see if she'd sold anything of Alice's? How could he even tell after all these years?

"So, I stopped by today to let you know that my attorney filed a dispute over the will this morning. I'm sure Phillip explained to you that all of Aunt Alice's assets would be frozen until the dispute is resolved."

Lucy stopped in the entry to the great room, her arms still crossed over her chest. Harper was right when she said that her brother would likely be the one to start trouble for her. "He did."

Oliver looked around at the art and expensive tapestries draping the windows before he turned and nodded at her. "Good, good. I wouldn't want there to be any awkward misunderstandings if you tried to sell something from the apartment. I'm fairly certain you've never inherited anything before and wouldn't know how it all worked."

"Yes, it's a shame. I was just itching to dump that gaudy Léger painting in the hallway. I always thought it clashed with the Cézanne beside it, but Alice would never listen to reason," she replied sarcastically. Calling a Léger gaudy would get her kicked out of the Yale art history program.

Oliver narrowed his gaze at her. "Which painting is the Léger?"

Lucy shelved a smirk. He thought he was so smart and superior to her, but art was obviously something he didn't know anything about. "It's the colorful cubist piece with the bicycles. But that aside, I was just kidding. Even if I win in court—

and I doubt I will—I wouldn't sell any of Alice's art."

He glanced over her shoulder at the Léger and shrugged before moving to the collection of cream striped sofas. He sat down, manspreading across the loveseat in a cocky manner that she found both infuriating and oddly intriguing. He wore his confidence well, but he seemed too comfortable here, as though he were already planning on moving in to the place Lucy had called home for years.

"And why is that?" he asked. "I would think most people in your position would be itching to liquidate the millions in art she hoarded here."

She sighed, not really in the mood to explain herself to him, but finding she apparently had nothing better to do today. "Because it meant too much to her. You may have been too busy building your computer empire to know this, but these pieces were her lover and her children. She carefully selected each piece in her collection, gathering the paintings and sculptures that spoke to her because she couldn't go out to see them in the museums. She spent hours talking to me about them. If she saw it in her heart to leave them to me, selling them at any price would be a slap in the face."

"What would you do with them, then?"

Lucy leaned against the column that separated the living room from the gallery space. "I suppose that I would loan most of them out to museums. The

Guggenheim had been after Alice for months to borrow her Richter piece. She always turned them down because she couldn't bear to look at the blank spot on the wall where it belonged."

"So you'd loan all of them out?" His heavy brow raised for the first time in genuine curiosity.

Lucy shook her head. "No, not all of them. I would keep the Monet."

"Which one is that?"

She swallowed her frustration and pointed through the doorway to the piece hanging in the library. *"Irises in Monet's Garden,"* she said. "You did go to college, didn't you? Didn't you take any kind of liberal studies classes? Maybe visit a museum in your life?"

At that, Oliver laughed, a low, throaty rumble that unnerved her even as it made her extremely aware of her whole body. Once again, her pulse sped up and her mouth went so dry she couldn't have managed another smart remark.

She'd never had a reaction to a man like that before. Certainly not in the last five years where she'd basically lived like her ninety-year-old client. Her body was in sore need of a man to remind her she was still in her twenties, but Oliver was *not* the one. She was happy to have distance between them and hoped to keep it that way.

"You'd be surprised," Oliver said, pushing himself up from the couch. He felt like he was a piece on display with her standing there, watching him from the doorway. "I've been to several museums in my years, and not just on those painful school field trips. Mostly with Aunt Alice, actually, in the days when she still left her gilded prison. I never really cared much about the art, but you're right, she really did love it. I liked listening to her talk about it."

He turned away from Lucy and strolled over to the doorway to the library. There, hanging directly in front of the desk so it could be admired, was a blurry painting, about two and a half feet by three feet. He took a few steps back from it and squinted, finally being able to make out the shapes of flowers from a distance. He supposed to some people it was a masterpiece, but to him it was just a big mess on a canvas that was only important to a small group of rich people.

Even then, he *did* know who Monet was. And Van Gogh and Picasso. There was even a Jackson Pollock hanging in the lobby of his corporate offices, but that was his father's purchase. Probably Aunt Alice's suggestion. He didn't recognize the others she'd mentioned, but he wasn't entirely without culture. Aunt Alice had taken him to the museums more times than he could count. It was just more fun to let Lucy think he didn't know what she was talking about.

When she blushed, the freckles seemed to fade away against the crimson marring her pale skin.

And the more irritated she got, the edges of her ears and her chest would flush pink as well.

With her arms crossed so defensively over her chest, it drew her rosy cleavage to his attention. In that area, she had the cute barista beat. Lucy wasn't a particularly curvy woman—she was on the slim side. Almost boyish through the hips. But the way she was standing put the assets she did have on full display with her clingy V-neck sweater.

"Irises are my mother's favorite flower," Lucy said as she followed him into the library, oblivious to the direction of his thoughts.

Or perhaps not. She kept a few feet away from him, which made him smile. She was so easy to fluster. It made him want to seek out other ways to throw her off guard. He wondered how she would react when she was at the mercy of his hands and mouth on her body.

"I've always appreciated this piece for its sentimental value."

When Oliver turned to look at her, he found Lucy was completely immersed in her admiration of the painting. He almost felt guilty for thinking about ravishing her while she spoke about her mother. Almost.

It wasn't like he would act on the compulsion, anyway. His lawyer would have a fit if he immediately seduced the woman he'd decided to sue the day before. He did want to get to know her better, though. Not because he was curious about her, but because he wanted to uncover her secrets. He knew what Harper and Aunt Alice had thought of her, but he was after the truth.

This sweet-looking woman with the blushing cheeks and deep appreciation of art was a scam artist and he was going to expose her, just like he should've exposed Candace before his father was left in ruins with a toddler. He was too late to protect Aunt Alice, but that didn't mean he couldn't put things right.

Turning to look at Lucy, he realized she was no longer admiring the painting, but looking at him with a curious expression on her face. "What?" he asked.

"I asked what you thought of it."

He turned back to the painting and shrugged. "It's a little sloppy. How much is it worth?"

"Your aunt bought it many years ago at a lower price, but if it went to auction today…probably as much as this apartment."

That caught his attention. Oliver turned back to the wall, looking for a reason why this little painting would be worth so much. "That's ridiculous." And he meant it. "No wonder my cousin Wanda was so upset about you getting all of Aunt Alice's personal belongings as well as the cash. She's got a fortune's worth of art in here."

Lucy didn't bother arguing with him. "It was

her passion. And it was mine. That's why we got along so well. Perhaps why she decided to leave it to me. I would appreciate it instead of liquidating it all for the cash."

Oliver twisted his lips in thought. It sounded good, but it was one thing to leave a friend with common interests a token. A half-a-billion-dollar estate was something completely different. "Do you really think that's all it was?"

She turned to him with a frown. "What is that supposed to mean?"

"I mean, do you honestly expect everyone to believe that she just up and changed her will to leave her employee everything instead of her family, and you had nothing to do with it? You just had *common interests*?"

Lucy's dark eyes narrowed at him, and her expression hardened. "Yes, that's what I expect everyone to believe because that is what happened. I'm not sure why you're such a cynical person, but not everyone in the world is out there to manipulate someone else. I'm certainly not."

This time, Lucy's sharp barb hit close to home. Perhaps he was pessimistic and became that way because life had taught him to be, but that didn't mean he was wrong about her. "I'm not cynical, Lucy, I simply have my eyes open. I'm not blinded by whatever charms you've worked on my sister and my aunt. I see a woman with nothing walking away from this situation with half a billion dollars. You had to have done something. She didn't leave the housekeeper anything. You're telling me you're just that special?"

The hard expression on Lucy's face started to crumble at his harsh words, making him feel a pang of guilt for half a second. Of course, she could just be trying to manipulate him like she did everyone else.

"Not at all," she said with a sad shake of her head. "I don't think I'm special. I'm as ordinary as people come. I wish Alice had explained to me and everyone else why she was doing what she did, but she left that as a mystery for us all. There's nothing I can do about it. You can take me to court and try to overturn her last wishes. Maybe you will be successful. I can't control that. But know that no matter what the judge decides, I had nothing to do with it. Just because you don't believe it, doesn't make it any less true."

Boy, she was good. The more she talked, the more he wanted to believe her. There was a sincerity in her large doe eyes and unassuming presence. It was no wonder everyone seemed to fall prey to her charms. He'd thought at first she wasn't as skilled and cunning as Candace, but he was wrong. She'd simply chosen to target an older, vulnerable woman instead of a lonely, vulnerable man. A smarter choice, if you asked his opinion. She didn't have to pretend to be in love with a man twice her age.

"You're very good." He spoke his thoughts aloud and took a step closer to her. "When I first saw you at Phillip's office with your big eyes and your innocent and indignant expression, I thought perhaps you were an amateur that I could easily trip up, but now I see I'm going up against a professional con artist." He took another step, leaving only inches between them. "But that doesn't mean you're going to win."

Lucy didn't pull back this time; she held her ground. "The mistake you're making is thinking that I care, Oliver."

"You're honestly going to stand there and tell me that you don't care whether you get the apartment, the Monet and everything else?"

"I am," she said with a defiant lift of her chin. Her dark eyes focused on him, drawing him into their brown depths. "See, the difference between you and me is that I've never had anything worth losing. If I walk out this door with nothing more than I came in with, my life goes on as usual. And that's what I expect to happen. To be honest, I can't even imagine having that kind of money. This whole thing seems like a dream I'm going to wake up from and I'll go back to being Lucy, the broke friend that can never afford the girls trips and expensive clothes her friends wear. Things like this don't happen to people like me, and the people in the world with all the money and power—people like you—are happy to keep it that way."

"You're saying it's my fault if you don't get your way?"

"Not my way. Alice's way. And yes. You're the only one in the family that lawyered up."

That was because he was the only one in the family with nerve. "Someone had to."

"Well, then, you've made your choices, Oliver, and so have I. That said, I'm not sure there's much else for us to say to one another. I think it's time for you to go."

Oliver raked his gaze over her stern expression and smirked. He didn't have to leave. She had no more claim on the apartment than he did at this point. But it was too soon to push his luck. Besides, the more time he spent with her, the softer his resolve to crush her became. The closer he got, the more interested he was in breathing in the scent of her shampoo and touching her hand to see if her skin was as soft as it appeared. He would have to tread very carefully where Lucy was concerned or he'd get lured into her web just like the others.

"I think you're right," he said, pulling away from her before he got even closer and did something he might regret, like kiss her senseless so he could feel her body melt into his. He walked through the

gallery to the foyer and opened the door that led to
the elevator.

"Until we meet again, Lucy Campbell."

Three

"I don't know why you insisted on me wearing this dress, Harper. It's a baby shower, not a cocktail party."

As Lucy and Harper walked up the driveway of the sprawling Dempsey estate, she looked down at the white strapless frock her friend had practically pushed on her. It had taken nearly two hours to drive out to the property where Emma had grown up, and Lucy had doubted her clothing decision the whole way. Why they couldn't have the party at the Dempseys' apartment in Manhattan, she didn't know.

Harper shook her head and dismissed Lucy's concerns, as usual. "That J. Mendel dress is perfect for you. You look great. It's always a good time to look great."

"You need to print that on your business cards," Lucy quipped.

Even then, she felt incredibly overdressed for a baby shower, but Harper insisted they dress up. It was a couples shower for their friend Emma and her new husband, Jonah. Since they were both single and the event was coed, Harper had got it in her head that they should look even cuter than usual, in case there were some single friends of Jonah's there as well. At least that was what she'd said.

"You need to remember you're not just the poor friend from Yale anymore, Lucy. You have to start acting like someone important because you are someone important. You were before the money, but now you have no excuse but to show the world how fabulous you are."

Lucy sighed and shifted the wrapped gift in her arms. "I'm still the poor friend from Yale and I refuse to believe otherwise until there's cash in my hand and in my bank accounts. Thanks to your brother, I may not get a dime."

"We'll see about that," Harper said with a smirk curling her peach lips.

Oliver had made that same face when he visited the apartment the other day. The brief encounter had left her rattled to her core. Thankfully, no one else had decided to drop in unannounced. But seeing that expression on her friend brought an anxious ache back to her stomach. She intended to get some cake in her belly as soon as possible to smother it.

"Who does a couples baby shower anyway?" Lucy asked. "Any guy I know would hate this kind of thing."

"Knowing Emma and her mother, this will be anything but the usual baby shower. It's more of an event."

Lucy paused at the steps leading up to the Dempsey mansion and caught the distant sounds of string music playing. Live music for a baby shower? They'd passed dozens of cars parked along the drive up to the house from the gate. "I think you may be right."

They stepped inside the house together, taking the butler's directions through the ornately decorated house to the ballroom. Lucy bit her tongue at the mention of a ballroom. Who, other than the house in the board game *Clue*, had an actual ballroom?

Apparently, the Dempseys.

They rounded a corner and were bombarded by the sound of a huge party in progress. Lucy was instantly aware that this was not the punch-and-cake gathering with cheesy baby shower games she was expecting. A string quartet was stationed in the corner on a riser. Round tables were scattered throughout the room with sterling gray linens and centerpieces filled with flowers in various shades of pink.

A serpentine table of food curved around the far corner of the space, flanked by a silver, three-tiered punch fountain on one end and an even taller cake on the other end. A mountain of gifts were piled onto tables in the opposite corner. There were easily a hundred people in the room milling around, and thankfully, most of them were dressed as nicely as she and Harper were.

Lucy breathed a sigh of relief for Harper's fashion advice. At least for some of it. Harper had tried to get her to wear a piece of Alice's jewelry—a large diamond cocktail ring that would've matched her dress splendidly, she said—but Lucy had refused. It wasn't hers yet. She wasn't touching a thing of Alice's until the deal was done.

"I think Emma's mother went a little overboard for this, don't you?" Harper leaned in to whisper. "I guess since Emma and Jonah eloped in Hawaii, Pauline had to get her over-the-top party somehow."

Lucy could only nod absently as she took in the crowd. Being friends with Emma, Harper and Violet in college had been easy because they'd all lived in their sorority house and their economic differences were less pronounced. After their years at Yale, they all returned to New York, struggling to start their careers and make names for themselves. It leveled the playing field for the friends. This was one of the few times she'd been painfully reminded that she came from a very different world than them. She tried to avoid those scenarios, but this was one party she couldn't skip. Even with Alice's fortune, she'd still be a nobody from a small town in Ohio that no one had ever heard of.

"I see someone I need to talk to. Are you okay by yourself for a while?" Harper asked. She was always good, as were all the girls, about making sure Lucy was comfortable in new settings that were second nature to them.

"Absolutely, go," Lucy said with a smile.

As Harper melted into the crowd, Lucy decided to take her gift to the table flanked with security guards. There were apparently nicer gifts there than the pink onesies with matching hats she had picked out from the registry. One of them had a sterling silver Tiffany rattle tied to the package like a bow.

Without immediately spying anyone she knew, she decided to get a glass of punch. At least she would look like she was participating in the event.

"Lucy!" A woman's voice shouted at her as she finished filling up her crystal punch glass. She turned around to see a very pregnant Emma with a less-pregnant Violet.

"You two are a pair," Lucy said.

"I know," Emma agreed with a groan as she stroked her belly. "Four weeks to go."

"I wish I only had four weeks." Violet sighed. "Instead I have four months."

Just after Emma and Jonah announced their engagement and pregnancy to the world, Violet had piped up with a similar announcement. It had come as a surprise to everyone, including Violet, that she was expecting. She and her boyfriend had been on and off for a while, but finding out she was pregnant a few weeks after she'd been in a serious taxi accident had sealed the deal. Her boyfriend, Beau, insisted he wasn't losing her again and they got engaged. The difference was that Violet wanted to set a date after the baby was born. She, unlike Emma, wanted the big wedding with the fancy dress and wasn't about to do it with a less-than-perfect figure.

"Speaking of how far along you are," Lucy said, "how did the ultrasound go?"

Violet's cheeks blushed as she turned to Emma. "I'm not announcing anything because it's Emma and Jonah's night, but I'll tell you both, and Harper when I see her. We're having a boy."

"Oh!" Emma squealed and wrapped her arms around Violet. "Our kids are going to get married," she insisted.

Lucy suffered through a round of giggly hugs and baby talk. Since Violet discovered she was pregnant, it had been all the two of them could talk about. Lucy understood. It was a big deal for both of them. She just felt miserably behind the curve when it came to her friends, in more ways than one. She hadn't even dated since college. Marriage and children were a far-off fantasy she hardly had time to consider.

"Darling." An older woman with Emma's coloring interrupted their chat. It was her mother, Pauline Dempsey. "I want to introduce you to a couple business acquaintances of your father, and then I'd like you and Jonah to join us up front for a toast."

Emma smiled apologetically and let her mother drag her away. Violet turned to Lucy with a conspiratorial look on her face. "So… Harper said you have some news."

Lucy twisted her lips in concern. A part of her didn't want to talk about Alice's estate until she knew what was going to happen. She didn't want to get her hopes—or anyone else's—up for nothing. Then again, keeping a secret in her circle of friends was almost impossible. "It's not news," she insisted. "At least not yet."

"I don't know," Violet teased. "Harper said it was huge. Are you pregnant?"

Her eyes went wide. "No, of course I'm not pregnant. You have to have sex to get pregnant."

Violet shrugged. "Not necessarily. I mean, I don't remember getting pregnant. I assume sex was involved."

"Yes, well, you were in a car accident and forgot a week of your life. I'm pretty sure that missing week included you and Beau making that little boy." Lucy was suddenly desperate to change the subject. "Any names picked out yet?"

"Beau wants a more traditional Greek name, but I'm not sold. I was thinking something a little more modern, like Lennox or Colton."

"Where is Beau, anyway?" Lucy asked. "This is a couples shower, right?"

"Yes, well, he's been working a lot lately. Finding out we were pregnant put him in a tailspin. He's been empire-building ever since. This isn't his cup of tea, anyway."

Lucy nodded, but didn't say anything. As a friend, she tried to be supportive, but she didn't like Beau. He and Violet argued too much and their relationship was so up and down. It was hard on Violet. He seemed to rededicate himself after her accident, and later, when he found out she was having a baby, but Lucy still worried about her friend. She wanted it to work out like the fairy tales claimed. But fortunately, with or without Beau, Violet would be fine. She was the sole heir to her family's Greek shipping fortune and could easily handle raising her son on her own if she had to.

"I'm going to sit down for a bit. My feet are swelling something fierce and I'm only halfway through this pregnancy," Violet complained. "Come find me in a bit. I still want to hear about this big news of yours."

Lucy waved Violet off and took a sip of her punch.

"Big news of yours?" A familiar baritone voice reached her ears just as her mouth filled with punch. "Do tell."

Lucy turned around and felt that anxiety from earlier hit her full force. She swallowed the gulp of punch before she could spit it everywhere and ruin her white dress. She wished it were spiked; it would help steel her nerves for round two of this fight.

Oliver Drake was standing right behind her with a ridiculously pleased grin on his face.

Oliver was willing to admit when he was wrong, and his prior opinions of Lucy's attractiveness were way off base.

Where had this version of Lucy been hiding? He had no doubt that Harper, his fashion-conscious sister, had gotten ahold of her tonight.

Lucy's dark blond hair was swirled up into a French twist with a rhinestone comb holding it in place. Her dress was white and cream—a color combination that on most women, brides included, made them look ill. For some reason, Lucy seemed to glow. It was off the shoulder, and with her hair up, it showcased her swan-like neck and the delicate line of her collarbones.

It was hard to focus on that with the expression on her face, however. The rosy shade of her lipstick highlighted the drop of her jaw as she looked at him in panic. She hadn't been expecting him here tonight and he quite liked that. Catching her off guard was proving to be the highlight of his week lately.

"This big news," he repeated. "I hope it's something exciting to help you get over the shock of inheriting, then losing, all that money."

At his smart words, her lips clamped shut and her dark brow knitted together. When she wrinkled her nose, he noticed that only a few of her more prominent freckles were visible with her makeup on. He found he quite missed them.

"You've got a lot of nerve, Oliver Drake! How dare you come to the party for one of my best friends, just so you can harass me! Is nothing sacred to you? Tonight is about Emma and Jonah, not about your ridiculous vendetta against me."

Oliver looked around at the dozen or so people who turned and took notice of her loud, sharp words. Apparently their banter was about to escalate to fighting tonight. He had no plans to cause a scene here, despite what she seemed to think. Reaching out, he snatched up her wrist and tugged her behind him. There were French doors not far from where they were standing, so he made a beeline through them and out onto the large balcony that overlooked the east grounds of the Dempsey estate.

"You let go of me!" Lucy squealed as he hauled her outside, the end of her tirade cut off from the guests inside by the slamming of the door. Thankfully, the weather was a touch too chilly for anyone to be out there to overhear the rest of their argument.

"Is nothing sacred to *you*?" He turned her question on her. "Stop causing a scene in front of my friends and colleagues."

"Me?" Lucy yanked her wrist from his clutch. "You started this. And they're *my* friends and colleagues, not yours."

Oliver noticed the palm of his hand tingled for a moment at the separation of his skin from hers. He ached to reach out and touch her again, but that was the last thing he needed to do. Especially right now when she was yelling at him. "Yes, you. And you don't get to lay claim on everyone inside just like you laid claim to my aunt's fortune. They're my friends, too."

"I didn't lay claim to your aunt's fortune. I would never presume to do that, even if I had the slightest reason to think I should get it. Despite what you seem to think, it was a gift, Oliver. It's a kind thing some people do, not that you would know what that's like."

"I am kind," he insisted. The collar of his shirt was suddenly feeling too tight. Oliver didn't understand why she was able to get under his skin so easily. He'd felt his blood pressure start to rise the moment he'd seen her in that little dress. And then, after he touched her… "You don't know anything about me."

"And you don't know anything about me!"

"I know that yelling is very unbecoming of a lady."

"And so is manhandling someone."

"You're correct," Oliver conceded and crossed his arms over his chest to bury his tingling hand. "I'm not a lady."

Lucy's pink lips scrunched together in irritation, although there was the slightest glimmer of amusement in her eyes. Could she actually have a sense of humor? "You're not a gentleman either. You're a pain in my a—"

"Hey, now!" Oliver interrupted. Ixnay that thought on the sense of humor. "I didn't come here to start a fight with you, Lucy."

She took a deep breath and looked him over in his favorite charcoal suit. He'd paired a pink tie with it tonight in a nod to Jonah's baby, but he doubted Lucy would be impressed by the gesture. At the moment, he wanted to tug it off and give himself some room to breathe, but he wouldn't give her the satisfaction of seeing him react to her, good or bad.

"So why are you here?" she asked.

"I'm here because I was invited. Jonah and I are friends from back in prep school. Did Harper not tell you that?"

"No, she didn't." Lucy looked through the window with a frown lining her face, then down at her dress. It was short, ending a few inches above her knee with a band of iridescent white beads that caught the light as she moved. "Although a lot of other things make sense now."

Oliver couldn't help the chuckle that burst out of him in the moment. "You actually thought I'd driven two hours out of my way just to come here and stalk you tonight?"

Lucy pouted her bottom lip at his laughter and turned toward the stone railing of the balcony. "Well…it's not like we've ever run into each other before this. You have to admit it seems suspicious that you keep showing up where I am."

He stifled the last of his snickering and stood beside her at the railing, their bodies almost touching. He could feel the heat of her bare skin less than an inch away. "Maybe you're right," he admitted.

Oliver turned to look down at her. She was wearing white and silver heels tonight, but even then, she was quite a bit shorter than he was. Outside, the flicker of the decorative candles stationed across the patio made the golden glow dance around her face, a game of shadow and light that flattered her features even more.

She met his gaze with her wide brown eyes, surprised by his sudden agreement with her. "I'm *right*? Did I actually hear you say that?"

"I said you *may* be right. Maybe I got all dressed

up, dropped a ton of cash on a registry gift and came to this baby shower in the middle of nowhere just in the hopes I would see you here."

Lucy turned away and stared off into the distance. "I don't appreciate your sarcasm. I also don't appreciate you accosting me at a party. I'm missing one of my best friend's baby showers to be out here with you."

Oliver turned toward her and leaned one elbow onto the railing. "You're free to go at any time."

She turned to face him with disbelief narrowing her gaze. "Oh yeah, so you can start something else inside? Or throw me over your shoulder and carry me off next time? No. We're finishing this discussion right now. When I go back inside, I don't want to speak to or even lay eyes on you again."

He looked at her and noticed a slight tremble of her lips as she spoke. Was she on the verge of tears? He wasn't sure why, but the idea of that suddenly bothered him. "Are you okay?"

"Yes, why?"

"You're trembling. Are you really that upset with me?"

Lucy rolled her eyes and shook her head. "No, I'm shivering. It's freezing out here. I'm not dressed for an alfresco discussion this time of year."

Without hesitation, Oliver slipped off his suit coat and held it out to her. She looked at it with suspicion for a moment before turning her back and letting him drape it over her bare shoulders.

"Thank you," Lucy said as reluctantly as she could manage.

"I'm not all bad."

"That's good to know. I was starting to feel sorry for Harper having to grow up with you."

"Oh, you can still feel sorry for her. I was a horrible big brother. I made her life hell for years." Oliver laughed again, thinking of some of the wicked things he'd done to his sister. "One time, when she was about eight, I convinced her that my father's new Ming vase was made of Silly Putty and would bounce if she dropped it onto the floor. She got in so much trouble. Dad wouldn't believe her when she said I'd told her that. He grounded her for an extra week for lying."

Lucy covered her mouth with her hand to hide a reluctant smile. "Why are you being nice to me all of a sudden?" she asked. "You're not here to fight with me, and yet you're out here making small talk with me instead of inside with Jonah and your friends. What's your angle?"

That was a good question. He hadn't exactly planned any of this. He'd just wanted to get her away from the crowd before they made a scene. Once they stopped arguing, he was surprised to find he enjoyed talking with Lucy. There was an understated charm to her. The longer he spent with her, the more he wanted to spend. It was an intriguing and dangerous proposition, but one that explained his aunt's bold decision. If he felt swayed by her, his elderly aunt hadn't stood a chance.

"I don't have an angle, Lucy." Or if he did, he wasn't going to tell her so. "I guess I'm just trying to figure out what my aunt saw in you."

Lucy opened her mouth to argue, but he held up his hands to silence her. "I don't mean it like that, so don't get defensive. I've just been thinking that if my aunt really did want to leave you half a billion dollars, you had to be a pretty special person." Oliver leaned closer, unconsciously closing the gap between them. "I guess I'm curious to get to know you better and learn more about you."

Lucy's nose wrinkled, but for the first time, it didn't appear to be because she was annoyed with him. "What do you think so far?" she asked.

"So far…" He sought out the smart answer, but just decided to be honest. "…I like you. More than I should, given the circumstances. So far, you've proven to be an exciting, intelligent and beautiful adversary."

Lucy's lips parted softly at his words. "Did you say beautiful?"

Oliver nodded. Before he could respond aloud, Lucy launched herself into his arms. Her pink lips collided with his own just as her body pressed into him. He was stunned stiff for only a moment before he wrapped his arms around her waist and tugged her tighter against him.

Kissing Lucy wasn't at all what he expected. Nothing about her was what he expected. She didn't back down from what she'd started. She was bold, opening up to him and seeking his tongue out with her own. Oliver couldn't help but respond to her. She was more enthusiastic and demanding than any woman he may have ever kissed before.

This wasn't the smart thing. Or the proper thing. But he couldn't make himself pull away from her. She tasted like sweet, baby-shower punch, and she smelled like lavender. He wanted to draw her scent into his lungs and hold it there.

But then it was over.

As she pulled away, Oliver felt a surge of unwanted desire wash over him. It was the last thing he needed right now—with Lucy of all women—but he couldn't deny what he felt. It took everything he had not to reach for her and pull her back into his arms again. He was glad he didn't, though, as his need for her was stunted by a sudden blow to the face as Lucy punched him in the nose.

Four

"What the hell do you think you're doing?" Lucy asked with outrage in her voice as she backed away from him.

Oliver didn't immediately reply. First, he had to figure out what the hell had just happened. He was being kissed one second, hit the next and now he was being yelled at.

"Me?" He brought his hand up to his throbbing nose and winced. It wasn't broken, but there was blood running over his fingers. He'd never actually had a woman hit him before. One for the bucket list, he supposed. "*You're* the one that kissed *me*!"

"I did not," she insisted.

Oliver frowned and sighed, reaching into his coat for his pocket square to soak up the blood. Harper had never mentioned Lucy being impulsive, but he was learning new things about her all the time. It had been ten seconds since their lips had touched and it hadn't been his doing. Surely she recalled that. "Yeah, you did kiss me. I said you were beautiful and you threw yourself at me."

Lucy must have been caught up in the moment, because she seemed very much embarrassed by the truth of his blunt description. Her skin was suddenly crimson against her white dress and she wasn't even the one who got punched. "Yes…well…you kissed me back," she managed.

What was he supposed to do? Just stand there? Oliver was not a passive man, especially when the physical was involved. "My apologies, Miss Campbell. Next time a woman kisses me, I'll politely wait until she's finished with me and hit *her* instead."

Lucy took a cautious step back at his words, making him grin even though he shouldn't.

"I'm not going to hit you," Oliver said, dabbing at his nose one last time and stuffing the handkerchief into his pocket. "I've never hit a woman and I'm not going to start now. Although it would be nice if you would extend me the same courtesy. What ever happened to an old-fashioned slap of outrage? You straight-up punched me in the face. You hit hard, too."

She twisted her pink lips for a moment before nodding softly. "I take kickboxing classes twice a week. I'm sorry I hit you. It was almost a reflex. I was…startled."

"You were startled?" Oliver snorted in derision at her Pollyanna act and immediately regretted it as his nose throbbed with renewed irritation. "How could you be caught off guard when the whole thing was your doing?"

"Was it?" Lucy asked. "You weren't complimenting me and moving closer to me with that in mind?"

Oliver didn't remember doing that, but it was entirely possible. Lucy had a power over him that he hadn't quite come to terms with yet. Despite his best intentions, he found himself wanting to be nearer to her. To engage her in conversation, especially if it might fluster her and bring color to her pale cheeks. He'd wondered several times, in fact, how it would feel to have her lips against his and her body pressed into his own. Unfortunately, it had all happened so suddenly just now that he'd hardly been able to enjoy it.

He wasn't about to tell her that, though. She might be a pretty, nice-smelling con artist, but she was still a con artist. She'd worked her magic on his sister and his aunt. He'd had no doubt she would eventually turn her charms on him to get him to drop the contest of Aunt Alice's will, and she'd tried it at her first real opportunity. Letting her know she'd gotten to him would give her leverage. No. Let her stew instead, thinking her plan hadn't worked and she'd flung herself at a completely disinterested man. She'd have to find a different way to get what she wanted.

"I didn't come to this party to see you and I most certainly didn't come to this party to try and seduce you. I can't help it if I'm a charming man, Lucy, but that's all it is. I'm sorry if you confused that with me being attracted to you."

Her mouth dropped open for a moment before she clapped it shut and pressed her lips into a tight frown. "That wasn't exactly the kiss of a man that wasn't interested," she pointed out.

Oliver could only shrug it off. "Well, I don't want to be rude, now, do I?"

Lucy balled her hands into fists and planted them on her narrow hips. "So you're saying you faked the whole thing just to be polite?"

"Yes. Of course." The arrogance of his response nearly made him cringe as the words slipped from his lips. Normally, he wouldn't speak to anyone this way, but Lucy was a special case. He wasn't handling her with kid gloves. She needed to know she wouldn't get her way where he was concerned.

Her brown gaze studied his face for a moment before she shook her head. "No. I don't believe you. I think you're just too arrogant to admit that you're attracted to me, of all people. That you could actually want the help. The trash that robbed you of your inheritance."

Oliver narrowed his gaze at her. She was good. Not only was she able to get under his skin, she was able to get into his head as well. That was disconcerting. He was the one who was supposed to be finding out all her secrets so he could expose her as a fraud, and there she was, calling him elitist in the hopes that his knee-jerk reaction would be to deny it and somehow fall prey to her charms to prove her wrong.

"We've established that we hardly know each other, Lucy. I'm not sure why you're so confident about who I am and what I do or don't think of you. But here… I'll prove to you that you're wrong."

He took two steps forward, closing the gap between them. Lucy stiffened as he got closer, but she held her ground. He had to admit, it impressed him that she didn't turn tail and run.

She wanted to, though. He could tell by her board-straight posture and tense jaw. "What are you doing?" She looked up at him with big brown eyes that were full of uncertainty.

She thought she could just call his bluff and he'd back down. No way. He was going all in and winning the hand even with losing cards.

Oliver eased forward until they were almost touching. He dipped his head down to her and cupped her face in his hands. Tilting her mouth up to him, he pressed his lips against hers. He wanted this kiss to be gentle, sweet and meaningless, so he could prove his point and move on with his night. He'd kissed a lot of women in his time. This would be like any other.

Or so he thought.

The second her lips touched his, it was immediately apparent that wasn't going to be the case. It was like a surge of electricity shot through his body when they touched. Every nerve lit up as his pulse started racing. The pounding of his heart in his ribcage urged him to move closer, to deepen the kiss, to taste her fully. In the moment, he couldn't deny himself what he wanted, even knowing his reaction played into her hands.

Lucy didn't deny him either. She melted into him, just as he'd expected. She wrapped her arms around his neck, her soft whimpers of need vibrating against his lips. Her mouth and her body were soft, molding to his hard angles. When she arched her back, pressing her belly against his rapidly hardening desire, she forced him to swallow a groan.

With her every breath, he could feel her breasts pushing against his chest, making him ache to touch them and hating himself for the mere thought. He wanted to press her back against the wall of the Dempseys' mansion and feel them beneath his hands. He was certain his father had felt the same way when he was swept up in Hurricane Candace.

This was getting *way* out of hand.

Oliver pulled away from Lucy at last, nearly pushing himself back although it was almost physically painful for him to do it. That simple kiss was supposed to prove to both of them that the other kiss had meant nothing. Instead, it had changed everything. Now he wasn't just curious about her as the woman who'd charmed his aunt out of a fortune. He wasn't just playing a cat-and-mouse seduction game. He wanted her. More than he'd wanted a woman in a very long time. His plan had clearly backfired in spectacular fashion, but he could still recover.

"See?" he said, taking another large step back to separate himself further and regain a semblance of control. He struggled to keep as neutral and unfazed an expression as he could, as though she hadn't just rocked his world in the midst of a stuffy baby shower.

"See what?" Lucy asked with a dreamy, flushed look on her face. She'd obviously enjoyed the kiss just as much as he had. On any other woman at any other time, that expression would've convinced him to swoop in again and push the kiss even further. Instead, he had to retreat before she caught him in her web for good.

"Do you see that you were wrong? That kiss was all an act, just like the first one. Honestly, it didn't do a thing for me." The truth was anything but, however he couldn't let her know that and think she had any chance of winning him over with feminine wiles.

Lucy's expression hardened as she came to realize that he was just messing with her and her plans had failed. Her jaw tightened and her hand curled into a fist again. Thankfully, he was out of her reach if she tried to take a swing at him a second time. "Are you kidding me?" she asked.

Oliver smiled wide and prayed his erection was hidden by his buttoned suit coat. "Not at all. I told you I wasn't attracted and then I proved it. That was skill, not attraction. Nothing more. Anyway, I'm glad we were able to clear that up. I wouldn't want there to be any other confused encounters between us. Now, if you'll excuse me, I'd like to get back in to the party. It appears as though they're about to do a toast for the new parents."

Lucy stood motionless as he nodded goodbye, brushed past her and headed back inside the ballroom.

What a pompous, arrogant jerk-face.

Lucy stood alone on the patio for a few minutes just to get her composure. The last twenty minutes of her life had thrown her for a loop and she just couldn't go back inside and act like nothing had happened.

First, she was too angry to return to the party. She knew she was flustered and red, and the minute one of the girls saw her like that, they would swarm her with questions she wasn't ready to answer. In addition, her hand was still aching from when she'd popped him in the face. She'd probably bruised her knuckles, but her only regret in hitting him was that it was premature. He'd certainly earned a pop in the nose with the nasty things he'd said later.

Second, she wasn't ready to run into him again so soon. It was a big room filled with a lot of people, but she knew that fate would push them together repeatedly until one of them surrendered and went home. The alternative was another fight, this one more public, ruining the party. She didn't need that. It was bad enough that whispers would follow about them being alone on the balcony together for so long. Or if they came back inside together. Or came back in separately.

There was no winning in this scenario, really. Tongues would wag and there had already been enough tongue wagging on the patio tonight. At best, she could make sure she was presentable before she went back inside.

Reaching into her small purse, Lucy pulled out her compact. Her hair and makeup were fine, save for her lipstick that was long gone. She wasn't surprised. That kiss had blown her socks off. Oliver could yawn and say it was as much fun as getting an oil change, but she knew better. She could feel his reaction to it in the moment. Men lied. Words lied. Erections…those were a little more honest. And his had been hard to ignore.

What was his angle, anyway? Yes, she'd kissed him. It was possible she'd read the signs from him wrong, but she really didn't think so. He responded to her. He held her like a man who wanted to hold her. But then he'd turned around and laughed the whole thing off like it was nothing and made her feel stupid for thinking it was anything else.

She felt the heat in her cheeks again as her irritation grew. Why would he toy with her like that? Was it because he was determined to think she was some sort of crook? Why couldn't he just get to know her and make up his mind that way instead of jumping to hurtful conclusions? Didn't he trust Harper's judgment at all?

Lucy finished putting on her lipstick and returned it to her bag. She might as well go back inside. If she waited until she wasn't angry any longer, she'd sleep out on the patio. Instead, she took a deep breath, pasted on her best smile and headed back into the house.

Apparently, she'd missed the toast. The string quartet was playing music again and the crowd had returned to mingling. Her trio of girlfriends were together and looked her direction when she came in the door.

Lucy stopped short in front of them. "What?"

Emma arched a brow at her. "Seriously?"

"I'm sorry I missed the toast. I had to get some air," she said, making a lame excuse so she wouldn't hurt Emma's feelings.

"Air out of my brother's lungs," Harper quipped.

Lucy froze. "What? How did you—"

"That's a wall of windows, Lucy." Violet pointed over her shoulder. "Anyone who looked that direction could see the two of you playing tonsil hockey on the veranda."

Lucy turned and realized that she and Oliver had been far more visible on the patio than she'd anticipated. She'd thought for certain that the dim lights of the patio and the bright lights of the ballroom would've given them a little privacy. "Uh, we were having a discussion."

Emma snorted. "Quit it. Just tell us what's really going on."

"Yes, is this your big news? That you're dating Harper's brother?"

"Heavens, no!" Lucy blurted out. "That…" She gestured back to the patio. "What you guys saw was just…"

"Amazing?" Emma suggested.

"A CPR lesson?" Harper joked.

"A trial run?" Violet tossed out.

"A *mistake*," Lucy interjected into their rapid-fire suggestions. "And when I tell you the big news Harper alluded to, you'll understand why."

"Let's sit," Emma suggested. "I'm worn out and I want to hear every detail."

They selected a table in a far corner that wasn't quite so loud and gathered around it. The girls waited expectantly for Lucy to start her story as she tried to decide where to begin.

"Alice made me a beneficiary of her will."

"That's great," Emma said. "I mean, it makes sense. You two were so close."

"Yeah," Lucy agreed. "There's just one problem."

"How could an inheritance be a problem?" Violet asked.

"Because she left me damn near all of it. About half a billion dollars in cash, investments and property."

The words hung in the air for a few moments. Emma and Violet looked stunned. Harper sat with a smug smile on her face. She was confident that all of this would work out. Perhaps because that was the kind of life she led. Things were different for Lucy.

"You said billion. With a *b*?" Emma asked.

Lucy could only nod. What else did you say to something like that?

"And why aren't you more excited? You didn't even seem like you wanted to tell us." Violet's brow furrowed in confusion. "You'd think you'd be shouting it from the rooftops and lighting cigars with hundred dollar bills."

That would be a sight to see. "I'm not excited because I don't believe for one second that it's going to really happen the way Alice wanted."

"And why not?" Emma asked.

"Because of Oliver," Harper interjected. "He's all spun up about the whole thing. The family is convinced that Lucy is some kind of swindler that tricked Alice into giving her everything."

"I swear I didn't even know she did it," Lucy said.

"You don't have to defend yourself to us, honey." Violet shook her head. "We know you better than that. If Alice left you that money, it's because she thought you deserved it. Who are they to decide what she could and couldn't do with her own money?"

"I think they're trying to prove that she wasn't mentally competent to make the change. She only did it a few months ago. It doesn't look good for me, so that's why I didn't say anything. I didn't want to get anyone's hopes up and have it all fall through. Oliver has a team of fancy attorneys just ready to crush me. Honestly, I don't think I stand a chance."

"So why, exactly, were you kissing Oliver on the patio if he's the bad guy?" Emma asked, bringing the conversation back around to the part Lucy had wanted to avoid.

Once again, the other three women looked at her and she was at a loss for words. "When I saw him, I thought he'd followed me here. He showed up at the apartment the other day and we argued. When we started to argue again, he pulled me outside so we wouldn't cause a scene at the party. Somehow... I don't really know how...we kissed. Then he kissed me a second time to prove that kissing me was meaningless."

"What happened to his face?" Harper asked. "He was all red when he came back inside."

"It might have been because I punched him in the nose."

Violet covered her mouth to smother a giggle. Emma didn't bother, laughing loudly at Oliver's expense. It didn't take long before all four friends were laughing at the table together.

"You seriously punched him?"

Lucy nodded, wiping tears of laughter from her eyes. "I did. And he didn't deserve it. At least not yet."

"Oh, I'm sure he deserved it," Harper added. "He's done something to warrant a good pop, I assure you. Taking Alice's will to the judge is cause enough."

"Do you really think he'll get it overturned?" Emma asked. "He doesn't even need the money. Jonah says he's loaded."

"He is," Harper said. "He's done very well with Daddy's business the last few years. But it isn't about the money, I'm pretty sure."

"Then what is it about?" Lucy asked. "Because this has been the most confusing week of my life.

I'm rich, but I'm not. I'm unemployed, but I may not need to work ever again. I'm homeless, and yet I may own a Fifth Avenue apartment. I'm applying to go back to Yale and finish school, but I may not even need to bother when I have an art gallery in my own living room. I've barely had time to grieve for Alice. Your whole family has a vendetta against me and I didn't do anything. I just woke up one day and my entire life was turned upside down."

Harper reached out and took Lucy's hand. "I know, and I'm sorry. If I'd thought for a moment that Aunt Alice was going to toss you into this viper pit, I would've warned you. But know it's not personal. They'd go after anyone. They all wanted their piece and they've been waiting decades for her to die so they can get their hands on it."

"What a warm family you have," Lucy noted. "I bet Thanksgiving was really special at your house."

"It's not as bad as I make it sound. Everyone had their own money, it's just that most of them were mentally decorating their new vacation homes and planning what they'd do with the money when the time came. Then nothing. In their minds, you yanked it out from under them, whether you meant to or not."

"Can't you talk some sense to Oliver?" Emma asked.

"I've tried. He's avoiding my calls. I think we just have to let the case run its course in court and hope the judge sees in Lucy what we all see. Once the judge rules in her favor, there's nothing any of them can do about it. But I didn't know he was bothering you, Lucy. If he shows up at the apartment again, you call me."

Lucy nodded. "I will." Looking around the crowded room, she was relieved not to see him loitering around the party. "But enough about all this. We're here to celebrate Emma and Jonah's baby, not to rehash all my drama. We can do that any day."

"I'm actually starving," Emma admitted. "Every time I think I should make a plate, someone starts talking to me or wants to rub my belly or something."

"Well, I'm pretty sure it's almost time for you to cut that beautiful cake. We can at least get you some of that to eat without interruption."

Lucy smiled as Emma's eyes lit up with excitement. "It's a vanilla pound cake with fresh berries and cream inside. At the tasting, Jonah had to take the plate from me so he could try a bite."

"Ooh…" Violet chimed in. "That sounds amazing. I've been nothing but hungry the last month. Beau keeps chastising me for eating too much. He says I'm going to overdo it, but I say pregnancy is my only chance to enjoy eating without feeling guilty. The baby and I are ready for some cake, too."

"Well, it's settled then," Lucy said. "Let's get these pregnant ladies some cake."

Five

"What are you doing here?"

Oliver could only grin at his sister's irritated expression as she opened the door to the apartment. A large portion of his life had been dedicated to goading that very face out of her. It was an unexpected bonus to the day. He hadn't actually been certain she was at Aunt Alice's apartment; he hadn't seen her since the baby shower the week before. But when he saw the Saks Fifth Avenue commuter van unloading downstairs, he knew that Harper was involved somehow. Where expensive clothes went, his sister was sure to follow.

"I saw the people from Saks unloading downstairs and I thought I would pop in to say hello. Personal shoppers coming to the house. It's as though someone has come into some money. Is that for you or for Lucy?" he asked, knowing full well that Harper was far too particular to let someone else shop for her.

"It's for Lucy."

Harper made no move to step back and let him into the apartment. Fortunately, the elevator chimed behind him and a well-dressed woman stepped out with a rack of plastic-wrapped clothing pushed by two gentlemen.

Harper's entire expression changed as she turned from her brother. "Hello, come in!" she said, moving aside to allow the crew in.

Oliver took advantage of the situation by going in after them. He happily took a seat on the sofa in the living room, waiting for what would likely be an interesting fashion show. After seeing what she'd worn the few times they were together, he knew Lucy needed a new wardrobe. Anything she wore that was remotely high quality was a hand-me-down from his sister. Honestly, he was surprised it took them this long to start shopping.

What would she buy first with her pilfered millions?

The two men from Saks left the apartment, leaving the rolling clothing hanger near the fireplace. He watched as the woman moved quickly to unwrap the clothes and present them to what she presumed was her wealthy client.

Lucy spied him the minute she entered the room, despite thousands of dollars' worth of clothes on display beside her. "What is he doing here?" she asked, echoing Harper's question.

Harper turned to where he was sitting and sighed. "I don't know, but it doesn't matter. We've got to find you an outfit for the gala. Perhaps a man's perspective will be helpful."

Lucy wrinkled her nose as she studied him and turned back to the clothing. "Harper," she complained, "these outfits are all way, way out of my price range." She picked up one sleeve and gasped. "Seriously. I can just wear something I already have in the closet."

"Absolutely not. You're a millionaire now and you have to look the part, especially at this gallery event. You want to work in the art world, don't you? This is your chance to make an entrance as Miss Lucille Campbell, not as Lucy, the assistant sent by Alice Drake. The invitation had your name on it this time, Lucy. Not Alice's."

Oliver watched curiously as Lucy shook her head and looked at the clothes. "How did they even know to invite me? I haven't told anyone about the money."

"Things like that leak out whether you want them to or not. I'm sure Wanda couldn't wait to share her outrage with her circle of friends and it spreads from there. The art world is small and people were probably eager to find out who would get Alice's estate. Honestly, I don't know how you've managed to keep it a secret."

Lucy pointed over to where Oliver was sitting on the couch. "That's why. He's why. You act like I already have this massive fortune, but I don't. All I have is what I saved to go back to school. I'm willing to spend some of that to get a dress for the gala, but not much. I have no guarantee that I'm ever going to see a dime of that money to replace what I spend."

"Will you at least try some of it on? You never know what you might end up liking."

"Yes, fine."

The saleswoman pulled out what was probably the most expensive designer dress on the rack. "Let's start with this one. Where would you like to change?"

She and Lucy disappeared down the hallway and Harper started sorting through the clothing on the rack.

This was an unexpected development. He thought for certain that Lucy would jump at the chance to buy some expensive designer clothes and start flaunting herself around Manhattan. Yes, he was responsible for putting a hold on the flow of cash from his aunt's estate, but there were ways around that. He was certain she could probably get a loan from a bank to front her lifestyle until the money came in. At the very least, charge up a credit card or two.

But she didn't. It was curious. She didn't seem to enjoy the position she was in at all, much to Harper's supreme disappointment. That woman loved to shop. Of course, so had Candace. She was full speed ahead the moment she'd gotten her hands on one of his father's credit cards. Candace had insisted that she just wanted to look as beautiful as possible at all times for his father. It was amazing how much money it took to make that happen.

Perhaps Lucy had a different angle. Her wide-eyed innocent bit was pretty convincing. Perhaps not spending money was part of it. Or maybe he was overthinking all of this.

He'd run through that night on the patio in his head dozens of times in the last week. Was she sincere? Did it matter? His body certainly didn't care. It wanted Lucy regardless of her innocence or guilt. Of course, his father had proved that following the advice of one's arousal was not always the best course of action. His dad had followed his right into near bankruptcy.

Speaking of what his groin wanted…

Lucy stepped back into the room wearing a gown. It was a sheer, tan fabric that looked almost as though she was wearing nothing at all but some floating tiers of beaded lace. It looped around her neck and when she turned to show Harper, it was completely backless.

"This one is Giorgio Armani," the saleswoman said proudly. "It looks lovely with your coloring."

The women talked amongst themselves for a moment before Harper turned to him. "What do you think, Oliver? If you're going to sit on the couch and gawk at her, you should at least make yourself useful."

It did look nice. He felt almost like a Peeping Tom, getting a look at her that he shouldn't have, but he'd rather see her in some color. "She looks naked. She could go naked for free. If she's going to pay that much money, she should at least look like she has an actual dress on."

Lucy laughed, clapping her hand over her mouth when she saw the saleswoman's horrified expression. Oliver was pleased that he'd gotten her to laugh, although he wasn't entirely sure why. She did have a beautiful smile. He hadn't really gotten to see it before. She spent all her time frowning at him, although he probably deserved that.

Harper just shook her head. "Okay, it's not my favorite either. Let's try this one," she said, pulling another gown from the rack.

"What are you dressing her up for?" he asked once Lucy disappeared again.

"The charity gala they're holding at the Museum of Modern Art Saturday night."

"Ah," Oliver said. "I got invited to that. Champagne, weird sculptures and people pressuring you to write checks. I bet the only reason they invited her was to get their hands on some of that money she's inheriting."

Harper put her hands on her hips. "And why did they invite you, hmm? The same reason. It's a charity event. That's the whole point. At least she knows what she's looking at when she walks around the museum."

Oliver shrugged off his sister's insult. It wasn't ignorance on his part when it came to art. He'd taken all the required art appreciation classes in college, as many class field trips as any well-educated child in New York, and followed Aunt Alice around museums on the occasional Saturday. He just didn't get it. Especially modern art. And if he didn't like it, why should he waste his brain cells remembering who this artist was or what that piece symbolized? He just didn't care. He could name maybe six famous painters off the top of his head, and four of them just happened to also be Teenage Mutant Ninja Turtles.

The saleswoman returned to the room looking very pleased with herself, but when Lucy came in behind her, she looked anything but. To be honest, this time Oliver had to hold in a chuckle. The dress was black with sheer fabric that highlighted the black structure of the dress like lingerie of some sort. On its own that would've been fine, but it also had red and pink cutouts all over it, looking like some kind of couture craft project.

"What on earth is that?" he asked.

"Christian Dior!" the saleswoman said with an insulted tone.

"No, just no," Lucy said, turning immediately to take it off. Apparently, she agreed with him.

"Is there anything on that rack that isn't a neutral or see-through?" Oliver asked. "I don't know what's wrong with color these days. The women are always wearing black or gray. Lucy should stand out."

The saleswoman clucked her tongue at him before turning to the rack again. "So no black, nude or white…" She flipped until she got to the last dress on the rack. "I guess we'll try this one, although it's not my favorite. The designer is relatively new and not very well-known."

"Give it a try," Harper said encouragingly. "You're not really helping us," she said to Oliver when they were alone again.

"It's not my fault her personal shopper picked out ridiculous outfits. I mean, you saw that last one, right? I know it's for a modern art event, but she doesn't want to be confused for an exhibit."

Harper's lips pressed together as she tried to hide a smirk. "Yes, well, this one is nice and I like it.

You'd better like it, too, or go home so we can do this without your help. Don't you have a business to run, anyway?"

Oliver shrugged. It was a well-oiled machine and at the moment, he was far more concerned with what was going on with Lucy. For multiple, confusing reasons.

When Lucy returned a moment later, Oliver struggled to catch his breath. The dress was a bright shade of red with cap sleeves and an oval neckline that dipped low enough to showcase her breasts. It fit Lucy beautifully, highlighting her figure and flattering her coloring with its bright hue. It had a sash that wrapped around Lucy's tiny waist, but other than that, wasn't particularly flashy. No beading. No lace. No sheer panels. No wonder the saleswoman hated it. If Lucy picked this gown, her commission would hardly be worth the trip.

"I really like this one," Lucy said. "Especially this part." She turned around and surprised everyone. The dress was completely open in the back, almost like a reversed robe that was held in place with the sash. It was paired with a pair of black satin capris.

Oliver wasn't even entirely sure if that qualified as a dress or a pantsuit, but he liked it. It was different and for some reason, he thought that suited Lucy. He liked the flash of skin along the whole length of her back. Any man who asked her to dance at the gala would get to run his palms over her smooth, bare skin. While he might enjoy that, he felt an unexpected surge of jealousy at the thought of her dancing with anyone else. Plus, the capri pants accented the high, round curve of her ass. He hadn't noticed before, but it was quite the sight.

When Lucy stopped preening, she sought out the price tag and sighed in relief. "This is the one," she said at last.

Oliver watched the women discuss the dress, tuning out the noise and noting nothing but the stunning vision in red. He hadn't intended on going to the museum gala on Saturday, but if Lucy would be there, in that dress, he might just have to amend his plans.

Lucy was fairly certain the woman from Saks Fifth Avenue was never coming back. There weren't nearly enough digits in the price of the dress she selected for the woman's taste. She just didn't see the point in spending thousands of dollars on a dress. A wedding dress, maybe, but not just some pretty outfit to wear to a party.

As it was, the price still seemed pretty steep—nearly a week's worth of her usual salary. But Harper was right; she needed to make a good impression on her first event out. Hopefully the inheritance would come through and she wouldn't have to worry about blowing that much on a single dress, but if not, she would be wearing that red outfit to every damn thing she could think of.

The apartment seemed to clear out all at once. The men returned and hauled the clothes out with a grumpy-looking saleswoman in their wake. Harper had an appointment and left soon after. That just left Oliver mysteriously perched on the couch when she went to change. She hoped by the time she got back, he would be gone, too.

Back in her own clothing—a nice pair of jeans and her favorite sweater—she returned to the room and found him sitting right where she'd left him.

"I still don't understand why you're here. Or still here, for that matter."

Oliver smiled and stood up. "I had some business on this side of town and when I saw the Saks truck, thought I'd pop in. Where Saks goes, Harper follows."

"And now she's gone," Lucy noted. "And you're still here. Want to ask me more questions? Hook me up to a lie detector this time?"

He strolled across the large Moroccan rug with his hands in his pockets. She tried not to notice how gracefully he moved or how he looked at her as he came closer. "Are you hungry?"

"What?" He'd completely ignored everything she asked him. How was she supposed to have a conversation with him when he did that?

"It's lunchtime. I'm starving. I'd like to take you to lunch if you're hungry."

She stood awkwardly, considering his offer for far too long. "Okay," she blurted out at last. If his sole purpose of coming by here was to uncover her dark secrets, he wouldn't find much. She might as well let him buy her lunch in the meantime. "Let me just grab my coat."

They walked silently out of the building together and downstairs to the street. Although they didn't speak, touch or even make eye contact as they strolled down the street together, she found herself keenly aware of his physical presence. Her body had somehow become attuned to Oliver, and the closer they stood, the harder it was for her to ignore even the tiniest of his movements or gestures.

Lucy was almost relieved when they encountered a more congested area and she had to drop back and follow his lead through crowds of people. The distance helped her nerves, at least until Oliver noticed she'd fallen behind. Without hesitation, he reached out and took her hand, pulling her back to his side. The skin of her palm buzzed with the sensation of his touch, making her whole body hum with awareness as though he intended to do more than just keep from losing her in the crowd.

Lucy expected him to let go once she'd caught up to him, but his grip on her held tight as they walked

a few more blocks to a restaurant she'd never been
to before.

"Do you like Korean barbecue?" Oliver asked as
he finally released her hand.

Lucy peered in the window and shrugged before
self-consciously stuffing that hand into her pocket.
"I don't know, but it sounds like an experience."

Oliver smiled and held open the door for them
to head inside. They were taken to a quiet table in
the back with a grill set into the center. The host
turned on the table and handed them both menus.
It didn't take her long to realize that Korean barbecue involved cooking the meat at their individual
table. When the waiter arrived, they selected their
drinks and meats. Oliver opted for a glass of red
wine and Lucy decided to stick with a soda. After
their last encounter at the baby shower, she wasn't
sure what to expect when she was alone with Oliver. There was no need to add alcohol to that mix.

Especially with her hand still tingling. Beneath
the table, she rubbed it over her jean-clad thigh and
wished the feeling away. She needed to keep her
wits about her when she was alone with Oliver. She
couldn't let her guard down no matter how much
she tingled or how he smiled at her. This might all
be part of his plan to undermine her claim on Alice's estate. She didn't know how, exactly, but she
refused to believe he just wanted to take her to lunch
to be nice.

The waiter arrived with their drinks, then placed half a dozen bowls on the table. There were different vegetables, rice and a few foods she didn't recognize. One had tentacles.

"Can I ask you something?" Lucy said once the waiter disappeared from their table. Her bravery where food was concerned was starting to wane, so she opted for a distracting discussion instead.

"Sure." Oliver picked up his glass of wine and awaited her question.

"I lived in that apartment with Alice for over five years. Harper was the only family member I ever saw visit, and in part, she was there to see me. I don't understand it. Why didn't you ever visit your aunt?"

Oliver nodded and focused for a moment on the wood grain of their table. There was an intensity about his expression when he was thinking that Lucy found intriguing, even when he was antagonizing her. He had the same look on his face when he was studying her. She didn't know what he saw or what he expected to see when he looked at her so closely. It made her uncomfortable, especially after those kisses on the patio, but she still liked watching the wheels turn in his mind.

"Aunt Alice didn't like having guests. You wouldn't know it if you went by, she'd treat you like royalty, but inside, she hated it. I missed her, and I wanted to see her, but I knew that it made her anxious, just like leaving her apartment made her anxious. So I gave her a computer, got her all set up and we emailed every day."

Lucy perked up at the last part. "You spoke to her every day?" How could she not know that? And why didn't she realize company made Alice uncomfortable? She'd never said a word about it to her.

Oliver nodded. "Aunt Alice was a complicated woman, although few knew it. Since you asked me a question, I'll ask you one. How much do you really know about my aunt?"

Lucy opened her mouth to answer, but when she thought about it, she realized she didn't have that much to say. "We shared a common love of art. She liked Chinese takeout from the place a few blocks away. She only drank hot tea with cream and one lump of sugar." There, she stopped. Most of the things she could think of were inconsequential, like being an early riser and watching *Jeopardy!* every weeknight.

"Now that I'm thinking of it, I guess she never really shared that much about herself. Not really. She never talked about her family or her childhood. I don't know if she ever worked or married or anything else. When I told you I didn't know anything about her will or how much money she had, it was true. We never talked about things like that."

"Aunt Alice never married," he began. "My father told me once, a long time ago, that she'd been in love with a young man in the forties. Unfortunately, he got shipped off to World War II right after they got engaged and never came home. She never dated anyone else, to my great-grandfather's dismay. He constantly thrust well-to-do men in front of her, hoping to secure business deals or strengthen ties, but you know her. She had none of it. I guess she never got over losing her first love."

Lucy sat back in her seat and frowned. "That's horrible. There's an old black-and-white photograph of a soldier in a frame beside her bed. That must be his picture."

Oliver nodded. "She got used to being alone, I think, and when everything else happened, she just decided it was better to be alone."

"What do you mean by 'when everything else happened'?"

"The terrorist attacks of September 11, 2001. It affected every New Yorker differently, but the whole thing really shook her up. She was supposed to go downtown to meet with a financial advisor later that morning. Then she turned on the news and realized what was happening. If her appointment had been an hour or two earlier, she would've been in the North Tower of the World Trade Center when the first plane hit. It scared the hell out of her. She never set foot out of her apartment again."

Lucy's jaw dropped as Oliver spoke. All this time, she'd been pointing fingers at him and his family for not visiting or even knowing Alice at all, when in truth, Lucy didn't know her either. Of course, she'd wondered why Alice never left the apartment, but it seemed rude to ask, so she never did. Some people developed agoraphobia without any particular incident at onset.

"What was she like before that?" she asked, suddenly curious about the friend and employer she knew so little about.

Oliver smiled, the sharp features of his face softening. "She was fun. After my mother died, sometimes my father would leave Harper and me with her for an afternoon while he worked. She would take us to the park or the zoo. The art museums, of course. She never worried about getting dirty or eating too much junk. As kids, we thought she was the greatest aunt in the world. It wasn't until we got older that we realized she was going out less and less. She was getting older, too, but I think she was feeling less comfortable out in the city. The attacks were the last nail in the coffin for her, I think. She decided it was safer to stay inside. And in time, she wanted less and less company, until she was almost completely closed off from the world."

"Why?"

"Fear, I guess. It's odd considering she seemed like the most fearless and exciting person I'd ever known. I sometimes wonder what she would've been like if her fiancé hadn't died. If she'd had a family. Would she still have closed herself off the way she did? I don't know. I hated it, though. I hated seeing that light in her extinguish."

The waiter appeared with their tray of meat and started to cook the first portion on the grill, effectively ending that line of conversation. Lucy was glad. Learning about Alice was enlightening, but also sad. There was a good reason why her employer hadn't talked about her past. She'd lost her chance at love and chosen to spend the rest of her life alone rather than be with someone else. Whether it was incredibly romantic or just sad, Lucy didn't know. But at the rate her love life was going, she might end up alone, too.

The server expertly flipped the meat, putting the finished pieces on their plates and explaining the different sides she'd been eyeing earlier. Once he was gone, they started eating and Oliver tossed a few raw pieces of Korean short ribs onto the grill to eat next.

Lucy watched him as he ate, thinking about their interactions since Alice died. She was a little ashamed of herself after everything she'd said and done. Yes, he was determined to prove she was a scam artist, but what did he know of her? Nothing. And she knew nothing of him. Or Alice, apparently. But she could tell that he had genuinely cared for his aunt. He couldn't fake the affection that reflected in his blue eyes when he spoke about her.

"Oliver, I want to apologize."

He paused, his food hanging midair on the end of his fork. "Apologize for what?"

"For judging you so harshly. For judging your whole family. All these years, I had this burning resentment for all of you. Sometimes I'd see Alice sitting in her chair looking at family photos and it ate me up inside that no one ever came to visit. She seemed so lonely and I felt like everyone had abandoned her for some reason."

Lucy shook her head and felt her cheeks start to flush with embarrassment. When she tilted her head up and looked him in the eye, the softness of his expression took away the last of her worries. She wasn't sure what she'd expected from Oliver, but it wasn't patience and understanding.

"That's why I lashed out at the reading of the will. When all these people showed up after her death, it felt like circling sharks drawn by chum in the water. Now I realize that it was how Alice wanted it. Or at least, how she needed it to be. So I'm sorry for anything ugly I said to you about all that."

Oliver held her gaze for a moment before smiling and popping a bite of food into his mouth. "It was an easy assumption to make," he said after swallowing. "I think we're all guilty of doing that to some extent, don't you?"

His gaze was fixed on her, with almost a pleading

expression on his face. He wasn't going to apologize for the things he'd accused her of, but maybe this was his way of acknowledging that perhaps he'd judged her too harshly as well. It didn't mean he was going to call off his lawyers, but maybe he wouldn't show up at the apartment to give her the third degree any longer.

"A truce, then?" Lucy asked, lifting her soda and holding her breath. While she would be glad to put an end to the fighting, she worried what could happen between the two of them without it keeping them apart. It was a dangerous proposition, but a part of her was anxious for him to say yes.

Oliver smiled and lifted his wine to clink her glass. "A truce."

Six

"Welcome, Mr. Drake. So good of you to join us this evening."

Oliver strolled into the Museum of Modern Art and stopped as he was greeted by a table of committee members organizing the charity event. The older woman who stood to welcome him looked familiar, but he couldn't place her.

"I am so sorry to hear about your aunt," she said. "She was a valued patron to the museum and the art world as a whole."

He nodded politely. "Thank you." Turning to the table where a young male volunteer was checking off guests on the attendee list, he leaned in.

"Can you tell me if Miss Campbell has already arrived?"

"She has." The young man beamed. Apparently he was a fan of her new outfit, too.

"Thank you."

They directed him up the short staircase to the second-floor atrium where the main portion of the event was taking place. At the top of the stairs, a waiter with a large silver tray offered him a flute of champagne, and he accepted. This type of event was not his idea of a good time, but at least there was alcohol involved. It helped to open people's pocketbooks, he was fairly certain.

The wide-open room with white walls that reached for the sky was dominated by a large pyramidal sculpture in the center. He was ashamed to admit he hadn't been to the museum since it had been redone years ago. A couple hundred or so people milled around the space, chatting and sipping their drinks. A band was playing in a corner of the room, but no one was dancing yet. The far wall was peppered with special pieces that his invitation said were being offered on silent auction to raise funds for the nearby LaGuardia High School of Music & Art and Performing Arts.

It didn't take long for Oliver to locate Lucy in the crowd. His eyes were immediately drawn to the crimson red of her dress that stood out amongst the sedate blacks, tans and whites of the people who accepted what the saleswoman pushed on them without question. The outfit looked equally stunning tonight, although now it was paired with elegantly styled hair, glittering jewelry and flawless makeup.

Altogether, it made for a woman he simply couldn't ignore. His body was drawn to her, urging him to cross the room and join her immediately. The only thing that held him in place was his desire to prolong the anticipation.

He enjoyed watching her chat with a couple about the large Monet that dominated an entire wall of the museum. Oliver could tell she hadn't spied him at the gala yet. When she knew he was nearby, there was something about her that changed. A stiffness, almost as though she were holding her breath when he was around. He wasn't sure if she was just more guarded, he made her nervous or if the palpable attraction between them simply caused her to be uncomfortable in his presence.

At the moment, she was sipping her champagne, smiling and speaking animatedly with a couple he recognized from other events around town. He liked watching her with her guard down. It was a side of her he'd never gotten to see, not even in the past when they'd called a truce or shared a kiss. That was his own fault, he supposed, but it made him want to know more about this side of Lucy. Perhaps it was the last piece of the puzzle he was missing.

Oliver watched as the couple finally dismissed

themselves to say hello to someone else, leaving Lucy standing awkwardly alone. She bit at her lip, the confident facade crumbling without the distraction of conversation. Now was his chance. He moved through the crowd of people to join her.

When their eyes met, Oliver felt a jolt of electricity run through him. Lucy smiled wide as he came closer, possibly relieved to see someone she knew. He could imagine that being in this situation and knowing almost no one must be quite intimidating. When she attended for Alice, she could fade into the background, but with that dress, she couldn't hide from anyone. A familiar face, even his, would be cause for excitement. Or maybe, just maybe, she was happy to see *him*.

"Good evening, Miss Campbell," he said with a wide smile of his own. Lately just the thought of her brought a grin to his face. As his gaze flicked over her beauty up close, he wished he hadn't waited so long to approach her. "You're looking lovely tonight."

Lucy blushed almost as red as her dress. "Thank you. I didn't expect to see you here this evening. I don't recall running into you at any of the events I attended for your aunt. I thought you weren't much of a fan of art."

Oliver shrugged. He wasn't about to say he'd only come because her might see her. "I'm always invited, but I usually have other engagements. Tonight was for a good cause and I had time, so I dusted off my tuxedo and came down."

Her gaze ran over his Armani tux for a moment with appreciation before she awkwardly turned away to glance at the art display across the room. "Have you looked at the pieces they have for sale tonight? There's some really lovely ones if you're looking to add to your personal collection."

"I haven't." The moment he'd seen her, the rest of the museum had faded into the background.

Oliver politely offered his arm and escorted Lucy to the other side of the atrium where maybe twenty-five paintings and sculptures were set up with silent auction sheets posted at each.

"Some of these were done by students at the school and others are donated by local artists. These kids show so much promise for their age. It's amazing."

He knew at this point he could let her arm go, but he didn't. He liked the feel of her against his side. A lot. "Did you ever have a desire to be an artist yourself?"

"Oh no," Lucy said with a nervous chuckle. "I love to look at it, to study it, but I can't draw a stick figure. I mean look at this one." She gestured toward a large painting of the Manhattan skyline with the Brooklyn Bridge stretching across the foreground. "This piece gets more amazing the longer you study it."

Oliver stepped closer to try to figure out what distinguished the piece from every other one they sold on street corners around the city. It was only when he got a foot or so away that he could see the image wasn't painted, but actually made up of millions of tiny hearts. Only from far away did the colored hearts make up the image of the city.

"The artist loves New York," Lucy continued. "The painting practically screams it. The color palette she chose, the light in the sky…it's a very well-balanced piece."

"It sounds like you really like this one. You should buy it," Oliver suggested. Part of him was waiting for her to start spending his aunt's money. Where was the joy in achieving one's goal when they couldn't enjoy it? He leaned in to look at the current bid. It was well within her means if the windfall went through. "It's only up to ten thousand dollars right now. If this artist is half as talented as you think she is at seventeen, this painting will be worth triple that one day. It's a great investment."

Lucy laughed off his suggestion and he realized how much he liked that sound. Arguing with her was fun, but he much preferred this version of his aunt's companion.

"You're just as bad as Harper," she said. "Counting chickens that may never hatch, no thanks to you. As far as I'm concerned, I have no money. Just some savings that have taken me the past five years to accumulate. I'm certainly not spending it on art when I may have no place to live in a few weeks' time."

Oliver felt a momentary pang of guilt. He'd taken the fun out of this moment for her. How different would it be tonight if he hadn't contested the will? Would he be the one there for her when she made her first big purchase? "But what if you did? What if you had all those millions at your disposal right now?"

Lucy's crimson-painted lips twisted in thought. "I haven't given it much thought. But in this case, since it was for charity, I would consider buying it. I would at least bid. But otherwise I would just feel too guilty spending that much money on something like that."

Oliver couldn't help a confused frown. He turned to look at her with a furrowed brow. "My aunt spent a hundred times that on a single piece. Why would you feel guilty doing the same? It's your money to spend however you want to."

Lucy pulled away from him and the painting and started toward the staircase that led up to other exhibits. Oliver caught up and took her arm again, in part to be a gentleman and in part because he liked the feel of her so near to him. The moment she moved from his side, it felt like a cold emptiness sidled up against him. He was eager to feel the warmth of her skin and smell the scent of her perfume again. It was a soft fragrance, like a garden after the rain, that made him want to draw it deep into his lungs.

"It's not my money," she said after quite a few steps. "It's Alice's money. And if by some stroke of luck it does become mine, I couldn't just blow it on whatever suits me. It was a gift and I need to cherish it. Do something good with it. Help people."

Curious. He'd never once spoken to someone who felt like money was a kind of burden of responsibility. Especially someone who'd schemed to get the money in the first place. "You could give it all to charity, I suppose. But Alice could've done that herself. She gave it to you for a reason. I wish I knew what that reason was."

Lucy stopped on the landing and turned to him with an understanding expression softening her features. "So do I. It would make things easier for everyone if she'd let us in on her little secret, don't you think?"

Her words rang true in Oliver's ears, making his stomach start to ache. Had he made the wrong call with her? He'd started spending time around Lucy with the intention of finding out what she was really about and all he'd uncovered was a woman who seemed kind, thoughtful, caring and intelligent. She was attractive as well, but didn't seem too concerned with that.

Either she was one of the greatest con artists he'd

ever met or he was way off base with this whole thing.

"This is my favorite part of the museum," she said, letting their prior discussion drop.

They had stopped on the surrealism floor. They started wandering through bizarre sculptures and even more bizarre paintings. "Your favorite, eh? Myself, I just don't get it," Oliver said, gesturing to the large painting hanging on the wall just ahead of them. "This one, for example."

Lucy sighed and stepped beside him. She studied the painting, but all he could focus on was the intriguing scent of her perfume and the glittering rubies at her ears. The sparkle drew his gaze to the long line of her neck. It was hard for him not to ogle, knowing the bare skin traveled down to the small of her back, exposed by the red dress she'd chosen from the personal shopper.

"This looks like something a child would doodle with crayons," he said.

"This is a popular piece by Joan Miró."

"Never heard of her."

"Him," she corrected. "This is part of his *Constellation* series from the early 1940s, and one of my favorites, actually. It's called *The Beautiful Bird Revealing the Unknown to a Pair of Lovers*."

Oliver forced his attention back to the painting and searched for whatever Lucy saw in it. He could find no bird, beautiful or otherwise, nor a pair of lovers. There was just a bunch of black circles and triangles scattered around a brown background with a couple random eyeballs. He turned his head sideways but it didn't help. It didn't make any sense to him. "Okay, Miss Art Connoisseur, show off your expertise and explain this piece to me."

"Okay," Lucy said with a confident nod. "This painting is well-known for its simplified color palette and line work designed to simulate a constellation in the night sky. What I've always appreciated about the piece is the sense of joy despite the chaos, which is a reflection of the artist's life at the time, in war-torn Europe. He worked on the pieces during the Spanish Civil War and actually fled the German advance into France with little more than this collection of paintings. He said that working on this collection liberated him from focusing on the tragedy of war. They were a joyful escape and I see that in his works. You have the calm of night, the jubilant dance of the stars…"

Lucy continued to talk about the work, but Oliver was far more interested in watching her. It was as though she was finally comfortable in her own skin, but it had nothing to do with him. She was no longer the fish out of water amongst the rich, mingling crowds of the charity event. She was the contemporary art expert, finally solid in her footing. Her dark eyes twinkled and her face lit up with excitement for the beauty of what she was looking at.

It was transformative. The dress was pretty, the makeup and the hair were well done, but it was this moment that Lucy truly became stunningly beautiful in his eyes. His breath caught in his throat as she gestured toward the painting and the overhead lights cast a shadow across the interesting angles and curves of her face. Her full, red lips moved quickly as she spoke, teasing him to come closer and capture them with his mouth.

"Oliver?"

His gaze darted from her lips to her eyes, which had a twinkle of amusement in them. "Yes?"

"You're not listening to a word I'm saying, are you? I've bored you to tears. You did ask me to tell you about it."

"Yes, I did. And I was listening," he lied. "I just got distracted by the beauty."

Lucy smirked and turned back toward the painting. "It is lovely, isn't it?"

"I was talking about you."

Lucy's head snapped to look in his direction as she gasped audibly. Her ruby lips parted softly as she looked at him without finding any words.

"You know, the last time I said you were beautiful, you kissed me. And hit me. But first, you kissed me."

Lucy's mouth closed into a smile. "Yes, well, I don't intend to do either of those things here, no matter what you say." She took a sip of her champagne and continued to stroll through the exhibit.

Oliver grinned and hurried to catch up with her. They'd just see about that.

"This section of the museum is dedicated to works of the sixties," Lucy said as they rounded the corner. She didn't want to keep talking about how beautiful he thought she looked tonight or about the kisses they'd shared at Emma's baby shower. Nothing good could come of the way he was looking at her, especially on the mostly deserted upper floors of the museum where anything could happen without witnesses.

She hadn't dated a lot, especially since she dropped out of Yale, so understanding men was not her strong suit. She got the feeling that even if it were, she would still be confused where Oliver was concerned. He didn't seem outwardly to like her, and yet he was always around. He was insulting her integrity one moment and complimenting her so-called beauty the next.

His mood swings were giving her whiplash. There was one thing she was certain of, however—those kisses on the Dempseys' patio had been passionate, tingle-inducing and toe-curling. Maybe the best kisses of her life. And yet his calm dismissal of the whole thing had left her uncertain of him and what he wanted from her.

Since Lucy couldn't be sure where she stood with Oliver, she knew her best course of action would be to keep her distance physically. Truce or no truce, it would only lead to trouble. She might not be able to avoid him when he seemed determined to seek her out, but she didn't need to encourage him. At least until the court case was decided either way, she needed to stay away from Oliver Drake.

She just didn't want to.

On the wall ahead of them was the famous collection of Yves Klein. She'd studied his work extensively in college as his artistic techniques were quite the scandalous production back then, and even now, although for somewhat different reasons. She was relieved to have art to talk about instead of focusing on the unmistakable connection between the two of them.

"I think you'll like this collection by Yves Klein. It's called *Anthropométrie de L'époque Bleue*."

Oliver stopped to study the first piece with a confused expression furrowing his brow. "I didn't understand the other one we discussed, but at least I could tell it was an actual painting that took skill of some kind. This is a giant white canvas with blue smears all over it."

Lucy smiled. "That's the final outcome, yes. But Klein was more of a performance artist in his day than just a painter. He created all these works with live audiences and an orchestra playing music in the background. He was quite famous for the events he put on. His most well-known piece, *Fire-Color FC 1*, sold at auction for over 36 million dollars in 2012."

His jaw dropped as he turned to look at her in disbelief. "I can't imagine why anyone would want to sit and watch a man paint for hours, much less pay that much for the sloppy outcome."

If that was all he'd done, it wouldn't have been interesting, that was true. She couldn't help leaning in and sharing the critical tidbit about Klein's methods into his ear. She pressed her palm on his shoulder and climbed to her toes to brush her lips against the outer shell. "He painted with nude women."

The lines in Oliver's brow deepened as he turned to her. "So he painted with nude women standing around? A little distracting and gimmicky, don't you think?"

"No. He didn't use paintbrushes. He didn't even touch the canvas, actually. He used what he called 'living brushes.' He literally used the bodies of beautiful nude women smeared in paint. Or he traced their naked bodies onto the canvas and burned the image into the fabric with a torch."

"Seriously?"

Lucy nodded. "I've watched video recordings of his exhibitions and they were quite the spectacle. Just imagine all these well-to-do art lovers coming to a museum, and when they get there, they're greeted by a man in a tuxedo and maybe six young, attractive and very naked women. They sat there and watched as the women smeared the paint all over their skin, then pressed their bodies into the canvas, just as the artist guided them. He was more of a director, really, coaching the women into creating the shapes and images he wanted to portray. With the music and the lighting…it was such a sensual experience. To capture that kind of feeling in a work of art is amazing, really."

He squinted at the canvas, but Lucy could tell he needed help envisioning it in the peculiar shapes left behind.

She stepped between him and the closest painting. "So picture me naked," she said with a smile. "There's buckets of blue paint and plastic tarps all over the floor. Even some canvases on the floor. I rub the paint all over my skin, covering everything as Yves directs, then position my body just so and press into the canvas." Lucy stood in front of the painting and tried to situate her body to mimic the imprint. "Can you see it now?"

He didn't answer. Finally, she dropped her arms and turned back to where he was standing. He was looking at her, but the expression in his eyes was not one of a casual appreciation for art. It looked as though he'd taken her far too literally when she'd told him to imagine her naked. A desire blazed in his blue-gray eyes as he watched her. So much for a distraction.

"I see it now," Oliver said, but he still wasn't looking at the painting. Instead, he took a step closer to her, closing the gap between them.

Lucy was suddenly very aware of her body. Despite the pleasant temperature of the museum, a blanket of goose bumps settled across her skin and made the hairs prickle at the back of her neck. She could feel the heat of Oliver as he hovered ever nearer, yet not touching her. The scent of his cologne made her long to press against him and bury her nose in his throat. All that talk about Klein's work had been the last thing they'd needed.

His hand reached out and his fingertips brushed across hers, sending jolts of electricity through her whole body. A warm rush of desire settled in her belly, urging her not to pull away from him this time. They'd both danced around this moment and she found she was desperate to see what would come next if they let things just happen.

Oliver leaned in, his face close enough to kiss her if either of them turned just right. "Lucy...?" he whispered.

She might be on a long celibate streak, but she knew what it meant when a man said her name like that. She wanted to say yes and throw her arms around his neck, but she wouldn't. This simmering passion just beneath the surface was dangerous, and she knew it. Did she dare give in to it? Could she trust the man who had previously been determined to call her out as a manipulative crook?

He certainly didn't seem interested in talking about his aunt's estate right now.

"Yes?" she replied, her voice trembling as her body ached to reach for him.

"Would you mind if we left the party a little early?" His breath was hot against her skin, sending a shiver down her spine.

"It just started," Lucy argued half-heartedly. It was a charity event and neither of them had been very charitable so far. "What about the school?"

Oliver leaned back and pierced her with his blue-gray gaze. "How about we go back downstairs, I write a check to make everyone happy and then you and I go back to my place. To talk about art," he added.

"A big check," Lucy suggested. He could afford it, even if she couldn't.

"Of course. You'll learn that with me, it's go big or go home," he said with a sly grin and a wink that promised more big things to come.

"4 for 4" MINI-SURVEY

We are prepared to **REWARD** you with 2 FREE books and 2 FREE gifts for completing our MINI SURVEY!

FREE
Value Over
$20!

You'll get...

TWO FREE BOOKS &
TWO FREE GIFTS

just for participating in our Mini Survey!

Dear Reader,

IT'S A FACT: if you answer 4 quick questions, we'll send you **4 FREE REWARDS!**

I'm not kidding you. As a leading publisher of women's fiction, we value your opinions... and your time. That's why we are prepared to **reward** you handsomely for completing our mini-survey. In fact, we have 4 Free Rewards for you, including 2 free books and 2 free gifts.

As you may have guessed, that's why our mini-survey is called **"4 for 4".** Answer 4 questions and get 4 Free Rewards. It's that simple!

Thank you for participating in our survey,

Pam Powers

To get your 4 FREE REWARDS:
Complete the survey below and return the insert today to receive 2 FREE BOOKS and 2 FREE GIFTS guaranteed!

"4 for 4" MINI-SURVEY

1 Is reading one of your favorite hobbies?
☐ YES   ☐ NO

2 Do you prefer to read instead of watch TV?
☐ YES   ☐ NO

3 Do you read newspapers and magazines?
☐ YES   ☐ NO

4 Do you enjoy trying new book series with FREE BOOKS?
☐ YES   ☐ NO

YES! I have completed the above Mini-Survey. Please send me my 4 FREE REWARDS (worth over $20 retail). I understand that I am under no obligation to buy anything, as explained on the back of this card.

225/326 HDL GMYG

FIRST NAME	LAST NAME

ADDRESS

APT.#	CITY

STATE/ PROV.	ZIP/POSTAL CODE

READER SERVICE—**Here's how it works:**

Seven

"Nice place," Lucy said as they stepped into his penthouse apartment.

Oliver just shrugged off the compliment. "It works for me. It's not a Fifth Avenue apartment overlooking the park or anything."

"Most people don't have that. Just because your aunt did doesn't make your place any less fantastic. If I hadn't been living with her all these years, I'd be renting a place the size of your entryway."

Lucy looked around in curiosity, taking in every detail of the place he'd paid to have professionally decorated. Oliver didn't really care about things like that. This was just a place to sleep at night. He did what was expected of him in this case because his apartment needed furniture and things on the wall. Thanks to all the money he'd spent, he now had expensive glass bowls that appeared to serve no real purpose and tiny statues that gathered dust. Thankfully he also had a cleaning service that came in to deal with that.

Oliver slipped out of his suit coat and threw it over the arm of the leather sofa. In his pocket, he found the receipt for the painting he'd just purchased at the charity event. He folded it neatly and tucked it away before Lucy could see it. She thought he'd simply made a donation to the high school before they left, but he'd actually gone in and placed a ridiculously high bid on the student painting she'd admired earlier. It ensured he would win the auction. Once the piece was assessed by the art department for the senior's final grade, it would be delivered anonymously to Lucy's apartment.

He wasn't entirely sure why he'd done it. Oliver wasn't exactly known for making flashy donations to charities or giving extravagant gifts. Most of the people in his life didn't need anything, so he quietly supported a few causes. In this case, however, he just knew he wanted to do something nice and unexpected for Lucy. She would appreciate it in a way few women he knew would. He hoped he'd be there when it was delivered so he could see the smile on her face when she saw it. That was enough for him.

ANDREA LAURENCE   115

"I see now why it's so easy for you to show up at the apartment unannounced," she said, pulling him from his thoughts. "You're only a few blocks away."

He approached her from behind as she stood in his living room and reached up to help her slip out of her coat. The night had grown chilly, but his apartment was very warm. He sighed as his eyes took in one inch after the next of her exposed back as the coat slipped down her arms and into his. The movement brought the scent of her skin to his nose, urging him to lean in closer. He longed to run his fingertip along the curve of her spine and follow the path with his mouth. Every time he looked at that outfit, he liked it more.

With the coat in his arms, Lucy turned to look at him expectantly. What had she asked about? Where he lived. "Yes," he responded. Oliver took a deep breath to push aside the building desire for a little while longer. He had no intention of attacking Lucy the moment he got her alone, as much as he might like to. "It's convenient to my offices and such. It's nice to live close to my father and sister as well. Dropping in on you so easily was just a bonus." He laid her coat across his own on the sofa. "Would you like a drink?"

"I would," she said with a polite smile. "Do you have a patio or a balcony where we could step out and enjoy it?"

He hesitated for a moment, not sure if he wanted

to share that part of his life with her. At least not yet. It was one thing to want to seduce Lucy, another entirely to open up his most private place. His apartment didn't have a traditional balcony; it had something much nicer that was very personal to him. He'd actually never showed it to a woman he was dating before, and he wasn't even sure he'd call this situation with Lucy *dating*. "Not exactly," he replied as he disappeared into the kitchen to stall his response.

"What does that mean?" Lucy asked as she turned the corner to join him.

He wasn't entirely sure why, but he'd always kept that part of his life very private. Maybe it was watching his father give over everything to Candace, only to have her ruin it. Maybe it was just keeping something for himself that he didn't have to explain to anyone else. Harper had only seen his garden once.

And yet, he wanted to show it off to Lucy.

He'd never felt that compulsion before, and it unnerved him that he wanted to show her, of all people. "I have a large rooftop patio," he explained. "It's more of a garden, really. That's where I go when I want to…get dirty and unplug." From life, from stress, from all the drama of his family. He found his center when he was up to his elbows in potting soil. It was hard to explain that to the other rich

CEOs who preferred racquetball, cigars and fine scotch to unwind.

"That sounds wonderful," Lucy said. "I'd love to see it."

Oliver worked on opening a bottle of wine and pouring two healthy glasses of chardonnay. He tried not to appear nervous about taking Lucy to see his handiwork. Surely he could manage to show it to her without letting her know how significant it was to him. "Sure. There's some great views from up there."

He handed her a glass and she followed him to a door in the hallway that looked like a closet, but actually hid a staircase up to the roof. Oliver took a soothing breath as he stepped out onto the patio with Lucy in his wake. "This is my retreat from the concrete jungle," he said.

Lucy's reply didn't come right away. Instead, when he turned to see what was wrong, he found her slack-jawed and wide-eyed. She looked around his garden as though she'd never seen anything like it in her life. And maybe she hadn't. He knew immediately that there was no way to hide how important this place was to him. It was obvious just by looking at it.

"I don't know what I was expecting," Lucy said at last. "Maybe some clay pots with petunias in them or something. But nothing like this."

That's probably because there were few rooftop

gardens like this in the city. He had trees and shrubs in huge planters along the edges of the roofline that made the garden feel private and secluded. There were twinkle lights wrapped through the branches and strung overhead, mixing with the stars. Pea-gravel pathways made a complicated pattern around raised flowerbeds where he was growing all manner of flowers and a few vegetables he donated to the food bank. Many of the plants would soon die back for the winter, but most were still showing off their foliage and brightly colored blooms.

"I had no idea you were a gardener. Harper never mentioned it. How did the CEO of a computer company get into something like this?"

"Few people know about it. Harper knows, she just doesn't mention it very often because she's afraid I'm going to make her come up and pull weeds or something." Oliver stuffed his free hand into his pants pocket and slowly strolled along the gravel path.

"It's funny you should ask how I got into it... When I was very young, my mother had a garden like this on their rooftop, and I helped her from time to time. I guess I got my green thumb from her. After she died, my father basically let her garden run wild. He didn't want anyone up there messing with her things. Years later as a teenager, I got the stupid idea to go up there and grow some weed. It was such a mess that I didn't figure anyone would notice, but my dad saw me sneaking out there once or twice and eventually busted me."

"As my punishment, I had to clean up my mother's garden and maintain it flawlessly for six months. By the time my sentence ended, I'd found I really enjoyed it. I chose this apartment in part because of the roof access. It's all mine and since it's taller than most of the nearby buildings, it's incredibly private despite being surrounded by millions of other people. The previous owners had just put some patio furniture out here, but I transformed it over the last few years into a place that I think my mother would've loved."

Oliver had no idea why he kept rambling on about the garden and his love for it. He'd never told this story to anyone, and yet Lucy's simple question had prompted a flow of words that even he hadn't expected. He didn't understand why she had this effect on him. There wasn't just an attraction between them, there was more. A real connection that he wanted to build and maintain beyond this nonsense about the will. That was the scariest part of all.

"Are there still places to sit up here?" Lucy asked as she leaned in to smell a large, dark red rose.

That was one of his favorites—the Mister Lincoln rose. It gave off an amazing perfume in addition to being a beautiful, classic, crimson rose. "Yes. If we follow the path around, we'll see the pergola where I've put up some furniture."

They walked along the trail lined with rose-bushes, gardenias and zinnias, to the trumpet vine-wrapped pergola on the south side of the building. It framed the best view from the roof, showcasing the ever-changing colors of the top of the Empire State Building. Under the pergola was a double chaise lounge that was perfect for sunbathing, naps or working evenings on the laptop with a glass of wine or scotch and ice.

"Wow," Lucy said. With the giddy grin of a child, she kicked off her heels and lay against the raised back of the chaise. She tugged up her dress to expose the cropped pants underneath and wiggled her pink painted toes in their newfound freedom. "This is amazing. I would spend every minute I had out here if I could."

Oliver smiled and settled onto the seat beside her. She'd jumped into the chaise without giving a second thought to getting her designer dress dirty and he appreciated that. "I don't spend much time just sitting here, actually. Maintaining the garden takes up most of my free time since I do it all myself. If I'm out here, I'm pulling weeds and repotting plants. Trimming back bushes and watering. It's a lot of work but it helps me keep my mind off of my worries."

Lucy sighed and snuggled against his shoulder as she took a sip of her wine. Oliver felt the heat of her body sink through the fabric of his tuxedo shirt and warm his skin. The feel of her so close made his pulse speed up. Suddenly, he had the urge to rip off his bowtie and tug her into his lap. He wasn't going to rush things tonight, though. There was no need to not take their time and enjoy it.

"And to think," Lucy said, "I assumed you were just some heartless workaholic with nothing better to do with your limited free time than screw with me."

That made him laugh out loud, chasing away his heated thoughts for a moment. Lucy just said whatever came to her mind and he loved that about her. There wasn't anything practiced or polished about her words. It was authentic and refreshing, even when it was mildly insulting.

"Well, I am a heartless workaholic, but I have plenty of things I could do with my limited free time. I simply chose to spend the time screwing with you because I…" Oliver turned his head toward her with his lips nearly pressing against her temple. "I like you, Lucy. More than I ever thought I would. Probably more than I should, if I were smart. But I can't help it. And I can't help wanting you."

Lucy was stunned to silence. It was one thing to say that they'd called a truce on their war over Alice's estate. It was another thing entirely for him to declare he wanted her while they were alone on a romantic rooftop patio. That was serious. That was the kind of statement that led to action.

So action is the course she took.

She set her glass of wine and small beaded black clutch on the table beside them and shifted onto her side to face him. His expression was different as he looked down at her in the glow of the garden's lights. The hard edge of his jaw seemed softer, the sharp glare of his blue eyes warm instead. Welcoming. And not just with need, although she could sense the tension of desire in the press of his lips into one another. There was something about being here, in this place that was so special to him, that had changed him or at least shown her a side of him she didn't know existed. She liked that part of Oliver. Liked him enough to throw the last of her reservations out the window where he was concerned.

"Sometimes the things we want aren't the smartest choices," she said softly. "But they're the chances you're the most likely to regret not taking. I hate having regrets."

Lucy followed her words by leaning in and kissing him. This was no desperate assault like their first kiss on the Dempsey balcony, but a sultry warm-up to something more. She melted into him as she felt his hands seek out her waist and pull her closer. His mouth parted and his tongue slid past her own. The caress sent a surge down her spine, making her skin prickle with goose bumps and her core throb with need.

She never expected to be here, in a place like this, with a man like Oliver. Despite her desire to make more of herself one day, she never wanted it to be because she dated up on the social ladder. Even though being friends with women like Emma and Violet exposed her to plenty of sexy, successful men, she didn't think for a moment they would be interested in her.

But Oliver was definitely interested.

His hands moved over her body, exploring and caressing each curve and hollow like he was trying to commit it to memory. When his fingertips brushed over the bare curve of her back and waist, she shivered from the sizzling heat of his hand against her skin.

"Are you cold?" He whispered the question against her lips. "Your skin is freezing. We can go back inside."

"I'm not cold. You're just hot." *In more ways than one*, she thought silently. "And I like it."

"Oh really?" He smiled and gripped firmly at her hip. "Then I think you'll like this, too."

Lucy let out a soft squeal of surprise as Oliver pulled her into his lap with a firm tug, guiding her to straddle him on the chaise. The position was much more comfortable than lying side by side and allowed her free access to his body with her hands.

She ran her palms over his chest with a naughty grin, feeling the hard muscles beneath the starched fabric of his shirt. "You're right. I like this as well. I'd like it better with some of this fabric out of the way."

She moved quickly to his tie and the buttons of his shirt. He didn't resist, he just closed his eyes and tensed his jaw as her hips slowly moved back and forth, teasing at his rock-hard arousal.

"Damn," he muttered under his breath.

His response to her made Lucy bolder. Once his shirt was unbuttoned, she pushed it open and ran her hands across the golden bronze ridges of his chest. He wasn't a soft, pale businessman who spent all his time indoors in front of a computer. Apparently gardening was hard work that he did without his shirt on and she appreciated that.

He lay mostly motionless with his eyes still closed as she admired the gift she'd just unwrapped. Her fingers traced the edges of his muscles, grazing over his sprinkle of dark chest hair and trailing the path it made down his belly to his belt. She could feel his stomach quiver beneath her touch as she moved lower.

Oliver could only tolerate that for so long, it seemed; as his eyes flew open, he reached out to cup Lucy's face and pulled her mouth to his own. There was an edge of frenzy when he kissed her this time, the slow, sensual kiss from earlier harder to maintain as the tension built between them. She didn't mind. She gave as good as she got, touching him and pressing into his caresses to intensify the pleasurable feelings that they sent through her body.

Lucy only felt a moment of nerves as Oliver's fingers unfastened the strip of red fabric that held on her dress. There was nothing beneath it but the black cropped pants that paired with the open-backed gown, so she would be fully exposed. She didn't want to act nervous, however. She didn't want Oliver to know how long it had been since she'd been with a man or how badly she didn't want to screw tonight up. So instead, she pasted on her most seductive expression—at least that was what she was going for—and let the gown slip down her arms to pool with the rest of it bunched up at his waist.

She bit at her lip as Oliver studied her bare chest with appreciation. She held her breath until he brought his hands up to cover her breasts and knead them gently. He groaned aloud with approval as she leaned into his touch.

Oliver let go of her only long enough to tug the fabric of her discarded dress into a ball and cast it to the vacant side of the chaise. That allowed them to get closer, and he took advantage of that by sitting up, wrapping his arms around her waist and capturing one of her hard, pink nipples in his mouth.

Lucy's head went back with a soft cry she couldn't hold in. For a moment, she looked around, expecting to feel exposed somehow, but the garden was incredibly private. She could shout, cry and remove every stitch of clothing she had on without anyone being the wiser. It was an unexpected turn-on, titillating the inner exhibitionist she didn't know she had.

She clutched the back of his head with her hands, burying her fingers in the thick waves of his chestnut hair and holding him close. She was so caught up in the moment, the feel of his lips on her skin, that she didn't realize she was moving backward until her skin made contact with the chaise.

Now Oliver was on top with Lucy's legs clamped around his narrow hips. He held himself up with his arms planted to each side of her as he looked down with a satisfied smirk. Pressing forward, he rubbed his firm desire between her thighs. The sensation shot through her like a fiery arrow despite the pesky pants they both still had on. Not for long.

Oliver placed a gentle kiss on her lips, then continued down her body. One on her chin, each collarbone, her sternum, each breast, her stomach... stopping when he reached her capris. Those were quickly unzipped and pulled down her hips along with the lace hipster panties she was wearing beneath them. For every few inches of skin he uncovered, he placed another kiss on her skin. Each hipbone, her lower belly, the tops and inside of her thighs, knees, calves, ankles.

And then she was naked. Totally and completely exposed, panting and trembling with the overwhelming sensations he was stirring inside of her. She ached for him to touch her center, to fill her with the hard heat he'd teased her with so far. But instead, he stopped moving altogether.

Lucy opened her eyes to see him kneeling between her legs with an almost painful expression lining his face. "What's wrong?" No woman wanted to finally take off all her clothes and have the guy freeze up like that.

"I don't have anything," he explained with a sheepish look. "Protection, I mean. To be honest, I wasn't expecting this to happen. Especially not up here. It's not an excuse not to wear anything. I wouldn't do that. I don't know why I didn't think of this sooner. I was just wrapped up in you…and now you're naked and so beautiful and I…"

Lucy smiled and leaned over to reach for her purse sitting on the table. There, she pulled out the duo of condoms she carried for emergencies. She'd never had an emergency in all the years leading up to now, but she knew better than to not be prepared. That was when bad decisions happened. "Here," she said, holding up the foil packets and saving him from the torture he was leveraging on himself.

Oliver took them from her, clutched them in his fist and grinned. "You're amazing. Thank God."

He leaned down and kissed her with a renewed

surge of energy. Oliver pulled away for a few moments and when he returned to her, the pants were gone, the latex was in place and he was poised between her thighs. "Now," he said with a grin as he looked down at her. "Where were we?"

Lucy reached between them and wrapped her fingers around his length. He groaned as she rubbed the tip of him against her moist flesh, teasing them both to the point of madness, then positioning him just at her opening. "Right about here is a good place to pick up, I think."

"You're right," he agreed before pushing forward into her warmth. He moved at an agonizingly slow pace, savoring every inch until he was buried deep inside of her.

Lucy gasped at the sensation of being so completely filled after all the years she'd gone without it. She suddenly wondered why she'd allowed herself to become so much like her agoraphobic older client while only in her twenties, but at the same time, she wouldn't have traded this moment for anything. If five years of celibacy earned her a payoff like this, it was worth it.

It was as though he was the perfect key for her lock. Everything from the way he touched her, to how he kissed her, the taste of his skin, to the scent of his cologne, couldn't have been more right. And when he started to move, the floodgates opened deep inside of her.

She clung to his back, gasping and crying out to the inky black sky overhead as Oliver thrust into her. They rocked together on the chaise, their movements more frantic and their muscles growing more tense as the pleasure started to build up between them.

"You feel so amazing," he growled into her ear. "I don't ever want this to end."

Lucy couldn't respond. She was past the point of rational thought with her climax barreling closer with every surge. All she could manage was a steady chorus of encouraging yeses. *Yes, keep doing that. Yes, I don't want it to end. Yes, this is what I've been waiting for. Yes, yes, yes.*

That's when it finally happened. Like a tightly wound coil inside her body giving way, her orgasm exploded through her. It pulsated through her core, radiating to every limb and making her head swim with pleasure. Her hips bucked against his, forcing him in deeper as her muscles tightened around him. The combination sent Oliver over the edge a moment later. He thrust hard, finishing with a low groan of satisfaction.

They lay together that way—weak muscles, throbbing parts and harsh, panting breaths—for what seemed like an hour, but it was only minutes. Too exhausted to move far but content in each other's arms, they finally untangled and righted themselves on the chaise to snuggle up together. Lucy nuzzled into the crook of his arm and molded to his side. Oliver tugged her voluminous red gown over them to shield their bare bodies from the night air and they fell asleep there under the ever-glowing Manhattan sky.

Eight

Making love to Lucy was amazing, but Oliver found he quite liked just talking to her as well. After a short nap on the rooftop, they got chilly, gathered their clothes and moved downstairs to his bed. There, he made love to her again, but instead of being sleepy, they were energized with conversation. They'd managed to lie in bed talking to the wee hours of the morning. He could tell she was getting tired, but like a stubborn toddler, not willing to give in to sleep quite yet.

"Harper and I are taking the train up to Connecticut next weekend," Lucy said.

"A fun girls trip?" Oliver asked.

"Something like that. Do you have any plans? Maybe we can do something when I get back."

Oliver picked up his phone from the nightstand to check his calendar. He would be lost without it. "Yep. I'm taking Danny to Coney Island. He's finally tall enough to ride the roller coaster and he's been pestering me for weeks."

"Who's Danny?"

Oliver frowned. Not at Lucy, but at the fact that he hadn't mentioned his brother to her in all this time. He supposed the focus of their discussions hadn't really been on his family aside from Aunt Alice. "Hasn't Harper ever mentioned our little brother?"

"Oh," Lucy said, the pieces almost visibly coming together in her mind. "Yes, she has, she just never uses his real name. She calls him Noodle for some reason. I honestly had no idea his real name was Danny."

At that, Oliver had to laugh. "His name is Daniel Royce Drake after my grandfather and my stepmother's favorite car, respectively. Harper has called him Noodle almost since the day he was born but has never told me why. Do you know?"

Lucy shook her head. "She's never said, and I guess I didn't ask. She just mentions doing things with Noodle or posts pictures with him on Snapchat every now and then. I have to admit, that's quite a nickname to grow up with."

Oliver shrugged it off. "I'm sure he'll be in therapy for far more serious things than a cutesy nickname his older sister gave him."

"Why would you say something like that? That's awful." Lucy frowned at him, wrinkling her freckled nose.

"It's true." Oliver's brow furrowed as he studied Lucy. Was it possible she didn't know the strange and sad tale of Thomas and Candace Drake? Surely Harper had mentioned it. She had just started at Yale when their father began dating Candace. Or perhaps Alice said something. Just because she didn't leave her apartment didn't mean she didn't know exactly what was going on in the family at all times. Or maybe Alice didn't know. At least to the full extent. Their father may not have wanted to admit he'd squandered his fortune on a beautiful woman.

"What could a little rich boy possibly have go wrong in his life to necessitate counseling?"

Only people without money would think that life was easy if you had it. Yes, the necessities of life were no longer a worry, but it came with a whole new set of troubles. Women like Candace being one of them.

"Nothing, now," Oliver admitted. "He was so young. I mean, I'm sure he misses his mother as a concept, but at the same time, she left when he was still a toddler. He may not remember much about her, only what's told to him. But eventually he's going to get old enough to realize that his mother used him as a pawn to get her hands on my father's fortune, and then dumped him when he wasn't useful to her any longer. When that dawns on him, it's going to hurt. And it doesn't matter how much Dad loves him, or Harper and I love him. It's going to make him question why he wasn't good enough for his mother to want him."

Lucy's big, brown eyes widened in concern, getting larger the more he said. "What kind of woman would leave her baby behind like that? That's horrible."

Her response and disgust seemed genuine. "A woman like my stepmother. Does Harper just not talk about our family at all?" he asked.

She shook her head. "Not really. I always got the feeling that talking about herself made her uncomfortable. I don't know why. Violet and Emma grew up with wealth and privilege like she did. I'm the broke outsider in the group."

"Not even when the stuff came up with the will? She didn't mention Candace?"

"No, she didn't."

Oliver sighed. He wrapped his arm around her shoulder and she snuggled in against his chest. "Candace is Danny's mother. My father remained single for over ten years after our mother died of cervical cancer. Mom's illness was hard on everyone, and when it was all over, he wanted to focus on raising us and running his company. There just wasn't any room left for a relationship, even if he had been ready to date again. After Harper went off to college, he met Candace and got all wrapped up in her. It all happened so fast. The whole situation was a nightmare from start to finish."

"Why was it a nightmare?"

"Because, for a start, she was three years older than *me*. Dad didn't seem to care about cradle robbing. She was beautiful and she fawned over him like he was the most amazing man she'd ever met. I guess he needed that after all those years alone. It was obvious to everyone but him that she was just after his money. He was blinded by her beauty and was so desperate to find someone to love him that he fell right into her trap. They got married within a year and she got pregnant with Danny pretty quickly. Before his second birthday, Candace had spent all my father's liquid assets and charged up all his credit accounts into the millions. When he finally put his foot down over her spending, it was only because he had no choice. She had wiped him out. He cut her off financially and she split almost immediately, leaving Danny behind. I guess he wasn't worth taking just for the child support checks when she could do better on her own. Last I heard, she married another tech billionaire from Silicon Valley. One of our competitors, if you can believe her nerve."

Oliver didn't want to drone on and on about Candace, so he got to the point as quickly as he could and waited to see what Lucy had to say about it. Very little, it turned out. Instead, they sat together in an awkward silence that seemed to stretch on forever.

Finally, Lucy spoke in a small voice. "So that's why."

"What do you mean?"

"That's why you automatically presumed that I'm an awful person. Because of her."

Now that he'd gotten to know Lucy better, he was ashamed to tell her as much, but he knew it was true. That's what experience had taught him. "I'll admit it colored my opinion, yes."

Lucy pushed herself up in bed and tugged the sheets to her chest defensively. She had a pained expression lining her brow and the corners of her mouth were turned down just slightly. "Colored your opinion, my foot," she snapped. "You didn't know me from Adam and you lashed out at me as though you'd seen a sketch of my face on a Wanted poster or something. You thought I'd conned your aunt just like your stepmother conned your father. Admit it."

"It's not—"

"Admit it," Lucy pressed. "You thought I was such a horrible person that I was willing to steal all your aunt's belongings out from under you all. Do you think I killed her, too?"

"Of course not!" Oliver replied. "Don't be ridiculous. Do you think I'd be lying in bed with you if I thought you were capable of something like that?"

"Okay, so not a murderer, but certainly a swindler."

Oliver twisted his lips in thought for a moment before he turned away from Lucy's accusatory gaze and sighed. "Okay, I guess I did. But you have to understand that the situation with Candace left me suspicious of *everyone's* motives, not just yours. On a date, the moment a woman asked what business I was in or what area of town I lived in, I could feel this anxiety start to creep in."

"Those are pretty common first date questions."

"I know," he said, feeling foolish about the whole thing but unable to suppress it. "But it felt like women were just trying to figure out how much money I had. Or if they knew my family and showed an interest, I convinced myself that it couldn't be because they were genuinely interested in me. Watching Candace work my dad over was hard. Especially since we couldn't say a bad word about her to him. Trust me when I say we tried, but he wouldn't listen. In the end, he looked like a fool and I never wanted to make that same mistake."

"So a woman couldn't possibly be interested in you because you're smart or handsome? Well dressed? Did you ever think that maybe one of those women was just interested in seeing if you had a big...garden?"

"I do have a larger than average garden." Oliver started to laugh, and then he clapped his right hand over his eyes in dismay. "Oh, you're right. I know you're right. I erred on the side of caution."

"And what good did it do you?"

Oliver looked down at Lucy, her naked body warm and curved against him. "It got you here, for a start. If I hadn't been so suspicious of you, I might not have followed you around and therefore, might not have fallen for your many charms."

Lucy smirked at him, unimpressed by his flattery. "And now that you've fallen for my charms... do you still think I conned your aunt?"

He knew this was a critical moment in the relationship he'd never expected to have with Lucy. After spending this time together, he should know, one way or another, if she was guilty of everything he'd accused her of. If he thought she was innocent, he'd say so right now without hesitation. And yet the seconds ticked by without his answer as he struggled with his prejudices.

Finally, he found the right combination of words. They might not be the ones she wanted to hear, but it was an honest response. "I really like you, Lucy. More than I ever expected to. I don't want to believe you could do something like that. I'm not sure if that makes me idealistic or just plain stupid."

Lucy watched his face for a moment. He could tell by the dimmed light in her eyes that he'd still hurt her even though she was trying to act as though he hadn't. "Thank you for answering that honestly," she said at last. She sat in deep thought for a few seconds before a yawn overtook her and he could tell she was losing the fight to sleep. "I don't know how to prove to you that I'm not like your stepmother, but I'm not going to figure that out tonight. I guess all I can do is keep trying. Good night, Oliver."

She leaned in to give him a kiss, then she lay back down, cuddling against him with another contagious yawn. After a few moments in the dark silence, he could tell she'd drifted off to sleep. He wished he could fall asleep that easily. But not tonight.

Tonight, he was left with questions he couldn't answer. Not with enough certainty to make him feel better. When Lucy called him out for putting his hang-ups over Candace on her and painting them with the same guilty brush, he felt foolish about the whole thing.

Oliver had decided Lucy was guilty without a stitch of evidence to prove it. And his big plan to uncover her secrets hadn't resulted in a single incriminating thing about her since that day at the lawyer's office. Honestly, he hadn't really tried. A background check hadn't revealed anything insidious. She was the only child of two blue-collar parents from central Ohio who split up when she was only a few years old. No criminal record, no negative remarks on her credit report...even her transcript from Yale proved her to be an above-average student.

By all accounts, she was delightful to be around, thoughtful, smart and sexy as hell. He couldn't imagine her being a crook like Candace was.

Even then, he had a hard time turning off his suspicious thoughts.

He'd like to think that if he truly suspected she was guilty of tricking Alice into changing her will, he wouldn't be in bed with her at the moment. That had to be worth something. And yet he hadn't called off his lawyers either. It was entirely possible that his aunt had simply left her estate to someone she thought deserved it.

As far as she knew, no one in the family was truly hurting for money. He was fine. Harper seemed to be getting along okay. And despite his father's claims of being broke, he was far from it. He still brought in more income in a single month from his investment portfolio than most people earned in a year. It didn't last as long in Manhattan as it would other places, but he wasn't about to be out on the street. He also had his retirement from the company.

Real estate holdings. It just wasn't enough to maintain the lifestyle Candace wanted.

His father may have been blinded by love, but Aunt Alice was no one's fool. If she could see all the quibbling going on over her will, she'd come back from the grave and tell them all to quit it because she knew full well what she was doing when she changed it. Lucy would have to be a very skilled scam artist to pull one over on her.

He didn't see that level of cunning in her. So why didn't he drop the protest? He was the only one keeping Lucy from getting everything she was due.

Maybe he would.

Oliver sighed and closed his eyes to try to sleep.

Maybe he wouldn't.

Lucy woke up in Oliver's bed the next morning. She wasn't sure if it was nerves or regret about last night, but she found herself wide awake at dawn with her mind racing over the night before. She didn't want to disturb Oliver, so she put on her capris, stole a T-shirt from his dresser and slipped out of the room.

She made herself a cup of coffee using the Keurig on his Carrara marble countertop, doctored it with half-and-half from his refrigerator and settled at the kitchen table. There was no reason she would be awake at this hour after staying up half the night, but there was an anxiety swirling in her stomach

and in her head. It demanded she wake up, so here
she was. There would no doubt be a nap in her future once she was back at her apartment.

For the time being, Lucy sipped her coffee. It
felt strange sitting idly in Oliver's kitchen, but she
felt equally weird about doing anything else in his
home while he was still asleep. That left her the option of leaving, and she knew that wasn't the right
path to take. Last night, while unexpected, had been
amazing and romantic. This morning might prove
awkward, and they might never share a moment like
that again, but it wouldn't be because she chickened
out and ran before he woke up.

Taking another sip of her coffee, she felt her
stomach start to rumble. Unlike her friend Violet,
who could charge through the day on a steady diet
of coffee and the occasional protein bar before she
got pregnant, Lucy liked to eat, and she especially
liked to eat breakfast. Eggs, pancakes, waffles, sug-
ary cereal, oatmeal, toast, bacon…you name it. She
was a fan of the meal in general. She wasn't the kind
who could make it to lunch without eating anything.

How long could she last today? She looked at
the clock in the hallway. It was just after six thirty.
There was a deli up the block where she could get
a bagel or order delivery, but she didn't need to be
seen by the general public. Especially not wearing
silk capris, a hole-ridden old T-shirt, no bra, last
night's makeup and morning-after hair. Lucy didn't

need a mirror to know that she'd announce "walk of shame" to anyone she passed.

Including Oliver.

On that note, Lucy pushed aside the idea of food for a moment and sought out the hall powder room to see how bad it really was. She winced in the mirror when she switched on the light. It was a rough look.

The clothes were what they were unless she wanted to wear her gown around the house, but she could clean up the rest. She splashed warm water on her face and used a disposable towel to wipe away the remnants of last night's smoky eye. Then she finger-combed her hair into a messy knot on the top of her head. It was still a far cry from her polished look at the museum the night before, but it was a casual, carefree messy instead of a hot-mess messy. The best she could do on an unplanned overnight stay.

The apartment was still silent when she stepped back out into the hall. Silent enough for her loud tummy rumbling to nearly echo. She couldn't put off breakfast for too much longer.

Lucy started rummaging through his cabinets for an easy option but found nothing she could grab like a pastry or a granola bar. That left real food. Oliver didn't strike her as the kind of man who did a lot of cooking, but she hadn't thought he was a gardener either. While the selection wasn't outstanding, she did find just enough between the contents of the pantry and the refrigerator to cobble together a decent breakfast for the two of them.

It was actually a dish that Alice had taught her to make in the years she'd lived with her. She'd called it Trash Casserole, but it was basically a crustless quiche filled with an assortment of breakfast foods. The idea was to make it with whatever was on hand, hence the trash, but Alice always made it following a strict recipe, which Lucy appreciated.

Her mother was an excellent cook after working at the local diner for twenty years, but it never rubbed off on Lucy. She wasn't a natural at it the way her mom was. Her mother could never explain how or why she did certain things, she just cooked it until it looked right and never followed a recipe. Eventually, Lucy just got frustrated with trying to learn and gave up.

Alice had been a lot easier to follow. She kept all her recipes on neatly handwritten cards in a brass box that sat in the cupboard. Those cards were gospel as far as Alice was concerned and she never strayed. Lucy had thought she would copy them all down for herself so she could make those dishes in her own home one day. Now, she realized, those painstakingly scripted cards were hers, along with everything else.

Maybe.

Lucy doubted that Oliver would begrudge her

some recipe cards if she really wanted them, but at the moment, they were tied up with about half a billion in other assets of the estate. She'd tried not to think about Oliver as her adversary, but his aunt's will was definitely the elephant in the room with them. Lucy didn't expect him to drop the protest just because they'd had sex, but a part of her hoped that maybe he knew her well enough now not to confuse her with his greedy stepmother. Or perhaps not. Sex somehow could change everything and yet nothing all at once.

"Something smells good."

Lucy looked up to see Oliver standing near the Keurig. He was looking deliciously messy himself, wearing nothing but a pair of jeans and some heavy stubble. The hard, tan stomach she'd explored the night before was on full display with his jeans hanging low on his hips. He ran his fingers through his hair and smiled sheepishly. The combination sent her pulse through the roof. It was nearly enough of a distraction to make her burn their breakfast if the timer hadn't gone off that very second.

"Good morning," she said, anxiously turning away from him and focusing on pulling the casserole out of the oven. "Are you hungry?"

"Mmm-hmm," he muttered as he came in closer and snuggled up behind her. He planted a kiss on her neck that sent a chill down her spine and a warmth of awareness across her skin. She turned to give him a proper good-morning kiss but realized his attention had shifted to what she was cooking.

"Is that Trash Casserole?" he asked with a look of astonishment on his face.

Lucy nodded. "It is. Have you had it before?"

"Have I had it before?" He took a step back and shook his head. "It's only the best thing Aunt Alice ever made. She cooked it every morning for Harper and me after we stayed the night with her."

She turned off the oven. "Well, good. She's the one that taught me how to make it, so hopefully it's at least half as good as hers."

Oliver eyeballed the dish with a wide grin. "It looks exactly like I remember it. I don't think I've eaten that in twenty years."

Lucy looked at him with a confused frown. "How is that possible? You had all the stuff to make it in the house. It's not a particularly complicated recipe. You mean you've never tried to do it yourself in all this time?"

He shook his head and took a step toward the coffee maker. "No. I don't cook. Not even a little. I pay a lady to come in twice a week to clean and stock the fridge with a few things I can eat. I found if I didn't do that, I'd just eat takeout until I needed bigger pants. Anything you found in the house, she left here, I can assure you."

Lucy wasn't surprised. "Well you'll have to apol-

ogize to her for me when she comes by again and
finds I've used up her supplies."

Oliver chuckled as he popped a pod into the coffee machine and turned it on. "She won't mind. I'm
sure Patty would be happy to come here and find
evidence of cooking instead of candy wrappers and
take-out containers in my trash can."

Lucy made them both plates and they settled together at the kitchen table. It was a nice moment to
share, diffusing any of the morning-after awkward-
ness. They were nearly finished when Oliver's cell
phone rang.

She sat silently as he answered, giving one-word
replies and frowning at the table. "Okay. I'll be there
shortly. I just got up."

He hit the button to hang up and looked at her
with an apologetic expression on his face. "That was
my dad. They're taking Danny to the hospital in an
ambulance. He had an accident at his riding lesson
this morning. I'm sorry to cut our breakfast short,
but I need to go meet Dad in the emergency room."

Lucy's soft heart ached at the thought of his little
brother at the hospital without his mother there to com-
fort him. She was hardly a suitable substitute—she'd
never even met the little boy Harper called Noodle—
but she couldn't go home in good conscience. She had
to do something to help. "I'll go with you," she offered,
getting up from the table with her dish in her hand.

He flinched at the suggestion, making her wonder if she was crossing a line by imposing on his family even after the night they'd shared. Was it too soon? Perhaps his father wouldn't want her there. He hadn't seemed any more pleased with her at the will reading than the rest of the family.

"You don't need to do that, Lucy. I'm sure he'll be fine."

She wasn't about to let him push her away that easily. "I know I don't need to do it, but I want to. If we can just stop by my place on the way, I'll do a quick change of clothes and I'll be happy to keep you company. It sounds like it's going to be a long day for everyone. I can fetch coffee or something. Let me help."

Oliver's thin lips twisted in thought for a moment, then he nodded with an expression of relief. "Okay." He stepped forward and pulled Lucy into his arms, dropping his forehead down to gently meet her own as he held her.

"Thank you."

Nine

Danny was a trooper. Oliver had to give him credit for that. He wasn't sure he'd have handled all of this as well when he was his age. He'd broken his wrist riding his scooter when he was nine and had been convinced at the time that no one had experienced his level of pain, ever.

Danny had four broken ribs, the doctor had said. X-rays showed the breaks were clean and would come together on their own. There was no risk for the bones puncturing the lungs. It sounded bad and it was quite painful, but it could've been much worse. During his riding lesson, the horse had gotten spooked by something. It bucked Danny out of the saddle, then stomped on his chest while he was lying on his back in the riding ring. He could've been killed in about four or five different ways, so some bruises and a few cracked ribs were a best-case scenario, really.

Dad had gone back to the apartment to get a few things. The doctors were going to keep Danny overnight. The first twenty-four hours were the most painful and where his breaks were located, he couldn't do much of anything for himself, even raise a juice box to his mouth.

That just left Oliver and Lucy with him for the time being, as Harper was out of town. Although Oliver had initially been thrown off by Lucy's request to come with him to the hospital, she'd been a lifesaver today. She'd brought them food from the cafeteria, magazines from the gift shop, and she even had a phone charger in her purse when their phones started to die from the constant calls and texts. Having her here had been nice. Nicer than he wanted to admit to himself.

Waking up with her, sharing breakfast together, even weathering a crisis together...every moment he spent with Lucy made him want to spend more and more. This was going to be a problem.

"Can I have a popsicle?" Danny asked. He was sitting up in his hospital bed with pillows propped up under his arms and a thin blanket thrown over his

legs. He looked so small in that bed, even smaller
than the seven-year-old usually looked.

Oliver got up from the chair, relieved to have a
quest to occupy his mind. "I'll go see what I can
do. Are you okay to stay with him?" he asked Lucy.

She nodded from her perch at the end of his bed.
"We'll be fine."

Oliver went down the hallway in search of a popsicle. The pain medicine was making Danny queasy,
so he wasn't much interested in the food they were
bringing him. If his baby brother wanted a popsicle,
Oliver would find him one. The nurses didn't have
any, just pudding and gelatin cups, so he headed
downstairs in the hopes of finding something in
the cafeteria or gift shop that would make Danny
smile. He'd hit a street cart if he had to.

He scored a Bomb Pop, finally, and carried it
back upstairs after about twenty minutes of hunting.
As he neared the doorway to Danny's hospital room,
the sound of voices made him pause. Danny wasn't
normally much of a talker, but the pain medications
had him chatting up a storm. He and Lucy were
talking and Oliver was curious about what the two
of them would discuss without anyone else around.

"The nurses cut off my favorite shirt when we
got to the hospital," Danny complained. "It hurt too
much to pull it over my head."

"I bet your daddy can get you another shirt just
like that one."

"Yeah, but it won't be the same. My mother sent me that shirt for my last birthday."

Oliver froze in place. He'd never heard Danny mention his mother. He hadn't even known she was in contact with her son until now. Dad hadn't said anything about it. For a moment, Oliver wasn't sure if he should be happy she was involved or mad for stringing his brother along.

"Did she?" Lucy asked in a polite voice that didn't betray what she knew about Danny's mother. "That was nice of her."

Oliver leaned forward until he could see around the corner of the door frame. Danny was still sitting up in bed. Lucy was sitting at the end of the bed, turned toward Danny with interest.

Danny shrugged on reflex and winced with the movement. "Not really. She sends a package on my birthday and at Christmas, but that's it. A *good* mom would do more than that. A good mom would've stayed around or taken me with her. Or at least visit every once in a while. That's what people say when they think I'm not listening."

He could see Lucy stiffen awkwardly in her seat. What did you say to something like that, knowing it was absolutely true but not being able to fix it?

"I'm sorry to hear that. Not having both parents around can be hard. You know, my daddy left when I was young, too."

Danny perked up. "Why did yours leave?"

Lucy sighed. "Well, I was small, so I don't know all the details, but my mom said he met someone else and started a new family. I never saw or heard from him again."

"Do you have more brothers or sisters?"

"Yes. Someone told me that I have two little sisters somewhere. I don't know their names."

Oliver couldn't believe how little he actually knew about Lucy's past and her family. What little he did know had come from the file on her the private investigator gave him. She never really talked about her life before she went to Yale and met his sister. Now he knew why. Being a single parent was hard. His father had enough money to get help when he needed it, never having to worry about bills or childcare, but the average mother on her own had no one to depend on but herself.

He imagined that drove Lucy to work even harder at everything she did. Getting into Yale was no easy feat, and getting a scholarship to cover most of the sky-high tuition was near impossible. He knew that having to drop out when she couldn't afford the tuition had to hurt. Being the companion of a wealthy old woman probably hadn't been her goal in life, but then again, that detour could very well make her richer than any Yale degree ever could.

"I just have Oliver and Harper," Danny said. "I've heard people say that's because my mom learned her lesson with me. I was a lot of work and

I ruined her body, she said. She got her shoes tied after I was born."

"Do you mean she got her tubes tied?" Lucy asked, stifling a chuckle at the seven-year-old's interpretation of the story he'd heard.

"That's it. I think." Danny sat thoughtfully for a minute, gazing down at the IV in his hand. "I'm sorry about your dad, Lucy. I guess my mom could be a lot worse. At least she sends nice gifts. She can afford to though, since she's married to a super-rich guy in California. I heard the housekeeper say that the guy invented a thing that's in every smartphone in the world. She wasted all of Daddy's money in just a few years, but I think it will take her a lot longer to spend all of the new guy's money."

Oliver was surprised to listen to how much his brother knew about Candace. He was young, but perhaps he wasn't as sheltered as Oliver thought. It sounded as though the grown-ups around him had the habit of talking about Candace as though Danny were too young to understand what they were saying. The knowledge seemed to steal a touch of his innocence too soon, but perhaps the truth wouldn't be as crushing as if he'd learned it all later. He was a smart, savvy little boy. Much more than Oliver gave him credit for.

He was also amazed at how deftly Lucy handled Danny. She was such a caring person, so unlike Candace. In a moment, she'd shifted the discussion away from bad parents and had Danny chatting animatedly about his favorite video game. Any bad emotions roused by their talk faded away as he prattled on about trolls and secret passages. Danny loved playing on any kind of gadget and would happily sit and get lost in a game for hours on end. Considering his family owned one of the largest computer companies in the world, it was probably in his blood.

Dad had actually forced Danny to take the riding lessons to get him out of the house. That had backfired a little, considering it had landed him in the hospital, but at least it had given him something to do that didn't entail cheat codes and warlocks. The next week of his recovery would be spent playing his game the moment he could hold up his own controller.

Lucy listened to him speak as though it were the most interesting conversation she'd ever had. She had that ability, that way of making you feel like you were the only person in the room. The most important thing in her life. No wonder Alice had been so taken with her. And Harper. And now, Danny, too. She was like a planet swirling around in space and pulling everyone else into her orbit.

He realized he was tired of fighting to escape her pull. The conversation they'd had in the late hours the night before had been enlightening for him. Danny's accident had occupied his mind for most of the day, but when he had a quiet moment, his thoughts always returned to Lucy. He had judged her unfairly. If he set all his prejudgments aside, he had no reason not to let himself fall head over heels for this woman. It was a leap he'd never risked taking before and he wasn't sure he was ready to do it yet.

But he could feel it coming. Before too long, the solid ground beneath him would crumble and he would have no choice but to fall hard for Lucy Campbell.

Oliver was startled from his thoughts by the drip of the popsicle onto his hand through a hole in the wrapper. He couldn't stand out in the hallway forever. Instead, he rounded the corner as though he'd just returned and presented the prize to the grinning little boy waiting for it.

After closing out the weekend at the hospital, the following workweek seemed to fly by. Lucy spent almost every evening with Oliver, returning to the apartment on Fifth Avenue when he left for work in the morning. During the day, she looked at apartments near Yale online and plotted out an itinerary for the trip she and Harper were taking up there the following weekend.

In all the time Oliver and Lucy spent together, they existed in a protective bubble—neither of them mentioning the fact that Alice's will was still pending a decision from the judge. They simply didn't talk about it, like an elephant in the room that they kept their backs to.

At this point, Lucy thought for sure that he should trust her enough to know she had nothing to do with the change in the will. And yet she didn't ask him to withdraw the protest and he didn't offer. They just carried on with their relationship as though the explosive events that brought them together initially never happened.

It lingered in the back of Lucy's mind, but at the same time, she was happy to ignore that aspect of their association. Things were so much better without that topic creeping into their conversations. She also tended to ignore the fact that she was planning on leaving Manhattan after the New Year to finish school regardless of what the judge decided. She hadn't mentioned that to Oliver either, and she didn't know why. Perhaps it seemed too early in the relationship to worry about the future.

If they were still together when the holidays rolled around, then it would be an important discussion. Now it would just be like putting a ticking time bomb out ahead of them, ready to blow their fragile relationship apart at its mere mention.

But would there be a better time, she thought, looking through the layouts of another apartment complex. Maybe.

Maybe not.

About six that evening, the doorbell rang and Lucy found Oliver standing in the foyer with sacks of takeout in his hands.

"What are you doing here?" she asked. "I was just getting dressed to come over to your place."

"I thought we could use a change of scenery," he said, stepping past her into the apartment. "I've also always wanted to eat in the formal dining room."

Lucy followed him curiously. "That's fine by me. What's so great about the dining room?"

Oliver set the bags down on the table, revealing some Italian dishes from a place close to his office. "When we were kids, we weren't allowed to eat in the formal dining room because we might spill on the priceless Moroccan rug. We had to eat in the kitchen where there was tile. When I was an adult, we didn't come over any longer, so I've never gotten to eat in here."

Lucy laughed. She'd honestly never eaten in this room either, but it was more out of convenience than anything else. When it was just Alice and her, it was easier to eat in the kitchen or to take a dish into her room and eat in bed by herself. "It's a first for us both then."

They settled at the table, eyeing the cream silk tablecloth, the infamous Moroccan rug and the large containers of pasta with red and white sauces sitting in front of them.

"Let's eat in the kitchen," they both said in unison, getting up and carrying everything out of the intimidating space as they laughed together.

When they were finished, Oliver grabbed the small container of tiramisu and two forks, and took Lucy's hand to lure her into the bedroom. "It's time for dessert," he said.

Lucy groaned as she followed him into her bedroom. She had eaten so much. She loved tiramisu, but she wasn't sure if she could stomach another bite of food. "I'm not sure I'm ready for dessert yet."

Oliver looked over his shoulder and gave her a coy wink. "That's okay. I think some physical activity first might make some room for more."

"Oh yeah? What do you have in mind?" she teased.

Oliver entered her room and set the container on the nightstand. Lucy came up behind him and ran her hands over his broad shoulders. She loved seeing him in his suits every day after work. She loved the contrast of the soft, expensive fabrics draped over the hard steel of his body.

He shrugged out of the jacket, letting it fall into her hands. She draped it over the nearby chair and they continued their familiar dance of undressing. It had felt strange at first to expose herself so easily to someone, and now her fingers couldn't move fast enough for her bare skin to touch his.

Oliver flung back her comforter and they crawled into bed together. He immediately pulled her body against his and captured her mouth in a kiss. It was amazing how quickly this had become like coming home to Lucy. It didn't matter where they were, being in his arms was what was important. The rest of the world and its problems just melted away and all that mattered was the two of them.

"I think I might eat some of the tiramisu now," he murmured against her lips, "if you don't mind."

Lucy did mind. They were in the middle of something and he wanted to stop and eat. But she kept her mouth shut and was rewarded for her patience.

He grabbed the container from the bedside table and carried it with him as he positioned himself between her thighs. Oliver kissed the inside of each knee before opening the container and filling the room with the scent of chocolate and espresso. He swiped his index finger through the cream on top and painted each of her nipples with it. Swirling more across her belly, he stopped at the satin edge of her neatly trimmed curls.

Oliver set the box aside and smiled widely at her as he prepared to enjoy his dessert. He licked a leisurely trail across her belly, circling her navel and climbing higher. Lucy squirmed with a mix of need and impatience, clutching at the sheets as he teased her. Finally reaching her breasts, his tongue teased at one tight nipple and then the next, sucking in the mocha-dusted mascarpone and swirling it around her skin with his tongue.

ANDREA LAURENCE   161

Lucy had never been someone's dessert course before and she found she quite liked it. The only downside to this arrangement was that she didn't have any for herself. When he picked up the box for more, she caught his wrist to stop him. "I want some, too," she requested sweetly and reached for it.

"I thought you were full," Oliver teased, holding the box out of her grasp.

She stuck out her bottom lip in a pout. "I just want a little taste. Please?"

"Well, since you said please…" Oliver dipped his finger in the dessert and offered it to her. She grasped his hand with her own, holding it steady as she drew it into her mouth and sucked every bit from his skin. When it was long gone, she continued to suck at him in a suggestive way that made him groan her name aloud with a hint of desperation in his voice.

"Okay. That's enough tiramisu for now," she said, finally releasing her hold on him. "I'm ready for the rest of my dessert."

"Very well," he said, tossing the carton to the far side of the bed. He lay down beside her. "Come here."

Gripping her waist, he pulled Lucy into his lap. She straddled him, feeling unexpectedly powerful as he looked up at her with a light of appreciation in his eyes. Lucy had never thought of herself as particularly pretty or having a good body—average at best—but Oliver looked at her like she was his fantasy come to life. It made her feel like maybe that could be true.

He brought his hand up to her face. His fingertips traced the curve of her cheek, then trailed across her swollen bottom lip. "You are so beautiful. I never want to close my eyes when you're near me."

How did this amazing man come into her life? Things had been so surreal since Alice died. The estate, the future…that was hard enough to believe. But Oliver—being with a man like him was beyond her wildest imagination. He was handsome, smart and successful. He was everything she'd dreamt of but never believed she would have. And yet here she was, straddling his bare hips and feeling his desire for her pressing against her thigh.

She sheathed him with a nearby condom, and shifting her weight, Lucy captured Oliver's firm heat and eased him inside of her. She closed her eyes and bit her lip as her body expanded and enveloped him. His palms cupped her hips and held her still. They both took a moment to savor the sensation of their bodies joining. Then at last, she moved her hips forward and back again, settling into a slow, steady rhythm.

They'd come a long way since that first day at the attorney's offices. It was hard to believe it had only been a few weeks since they'd met for the first time. Now she could hardly imagine her life without him. Just the thought was enough to make her chest ache in a way she could hardly describe. She'd never felt anything like that before. Lucy had spent more than one night lying in bed beside him, wondering what it could mean.

But now as she looked down at Oliver, she knew the truth of it—she was in love with him.

Did that mean she was making love to him for the first time? The realization intensified the sensations already building inside of her. She'd had a few partners in her life, but nothing she would call serious. Nothing that created the kind of emotional bond to the other person the way this did. This knowledge changed everything and she could feel it down to her core.

The pleasure started rippling through her, radiating from deep inside. She could feel her muscles tighten around him as her body tensed and prepared for her much-needed release.

"Yes," Oliver coaxed, his fingertips pressing into the flesh of her hips. "Give in to it."

It was a demand she couldn't help but follow. Her orgasm exploded through her like a shockwave. She gasped and cried out to the ceiling as the sensations pulsated through her like never before. Even as the pleasure filled her, it was the warmth in her chest that truly gripped her. That feeling of peace and happiness being here with Oliver seemed to envelop her. She bit her lip and savored it, even as

Oliver's hoarse groans began to mingle with her panting breaths.

She collapsed beside him in exhaustion and contentment. After a moment, Oliver gave her a soft kiss. "I'm going to go get a drink from the kitchen. Do you want anything?"

Lucy shook her head. She had everything she wanted in this moment. It couldn't be more perfect. As she watched Oliver and his perfectly round tush saunter out of the bedroom, all she could think of, all she could feel, was this overwhelming sense of love. She loved him. Really, truly.

She hoped that wasn't a huge mistake.

Ten

"I don't understand why we're back in Connecticut looking at apartments," Harper complained.

"I'm too old to live in a dorm or a sorority house," Lucy explained. "If I'm going back to school, I'm getting my own place near campus."

It was a cool, crisp day in New Haven. Summer had lingered longer than expected this year and the first signs of fall were finally arriving even though it was late September. Soon it would be time for changing leaves, oversize sweaters and boots. And when she started in the spring term this January, she would've moved on to heavy coats, hats, scarves and gloves.

"I really don't know why you're bothering with any of this. I mean, once the inheritance goes through, do you really need to worry about going back to school? You don't have to work another day in your life if you don't want to, much less move into a cheap off-campus apartment with loud jocks living upstairs."

Lucy could only shake her head and look at the map of nearby apartments she'd been given by the campus housing office. No, moving from a Fifth Avenue apartment to one of these places wasn't ideal, but it was reality. No one else seemed to be functioning in reality except her.

"This has got nothing to do with my inheritance. Whether I get it or not, I want to finish my art history degree. That's been my plan all along. When I dropped out, it was so disappointing. I've saved up all these years to pay for school, and with Alice gone, now is my chance. If that means an old apartment with shag carpeting and a run-down laundromat I have to share with a hundred other residents, so be it."

Harper halted her complaints as they approached the closest of the rental complexes near campus. "This doesn't look too bad," Lucy said. "Since it's so close, it's probably the most sought after and expensive place, too."

They found the front office and the manager walked them to an empty one-bedroom apartment they could tour.

"I've got a one-bedroom just like this one coming up after the fall term," the manager explained. "They're graduating and moving out before the holidays. I have a couple two-bedroom apartments coming up, too. Any chance you would be interested in one of those?"

"No thanks," Lucy replied. She'd basically lived in a bedroom the last five years and a shared sorority bedroom the years before that. Spreading out into her own apartment would be luxurious. "It's just me. I'm not interested in roommates."

"Okay. Go ahead and look around. I'll be here if you have any questions."

Lucy and Harper stepped inside and she breathed a sigh of relief. It wasn't that bad at all. To the left, there was a spacious living room with a patio. To the right, a dining room and the kitchen. Down a short hallway was the bedroom and bathroom. The fixtures weren't the newest and fanciest, but it looked clean and well maintained.

"I could make this work."

Harper wrinkled her nose. "Have you considered buying a condo or a townhouse instead?"

"With what money?" Lucy asked. "I swear you rich people can't quite come to terms with what it's like to be broke. After I pay for classes, books and fees, I'll have just enough for this apartment and food. That's it. I can't pull a down payment out of my rear end." She held up her finger to silence her friend. "And don't you dare bring up the inheritance again. I haven't heard two words from the attorney since Oliver filed a dispute. I can't plan my life around money that may never arrive."

Harper sighed and crossed her arms over her chest. "Okay, fine. What about Oliver then?"

Lucy frowned. "What about Oliver?"

"You two are…together. Dating? Whatever you want to call it. Things seem to be pretty good between the two of you. Are you really going to want to leave him behind in the city come January?"

That was something Lucy had tried to ignore. Not even her recent emotional revelation had changed that. Her plan before Oliver was to go to school and her plan remained the same. "We're hardly in what you would call 'a relationship.' Certainly not a serious enough relationship for me to give up my dream in order to be with him."

"I don't know. It hasn't been long, but you two seem pretty serious. It might not be love yet, but at the very least you're twitterpated."

"Twitter-what?"

"Twitterpated," Harper explained. "It's from the movie *Bambi*. It means you're infatuated. Maybe not 'in love' yet, but excited and optimistic and definitely 'in like.'"

Lucy ignored her observation and turned to study the appliances in the kitchen.

"You could transfer to another school that's in

the city. Columbia? NYU? You don't have to go back to Yale."

Lucy turned to Harper with her hands planted on her hips. "I worked hard to get accepted to Yale and I want that degree framed on my wall with Yale University emblazoned across the top of it."

Harper didn't seem convinced. "It's not as though the schools I mentioned are community colleges, you know."

"Yeah, I know. But before Oliver or money came into the picture, I made plans to come back here. I'm already registered for the spring. It's happening. So are you going to help me find a place to live or complain the whole time?"

She rolled her eyes and pasted on a smile. "I'm going to help you find an apartment in New Haven because I'm a supportive friend who loves you."

"Good. Let's go."

They walked out of the apartment together with a brochure from the manager and her card to call when Lucy made a decision. They toured two more apartment complexes before they went to Vito's Deli, one of their former college haunts, for lunch.

"I'm starving," Harper declared as they lined up at the counter to place their order.

Lucy had loved this shop when they were in school, but suddenly, the idea of it wasn't as exciting as it used to be. The smell of meat and pickles hit her like a blast of unwelcome air when they walked inside. She hadn't been feeling great the last couple of days, but she figured it was something she'd eaten. Now she wasn't so sure.

"Lucy, are you okay?"

She turned her head to her friend. "Why?"

Harper cocked her head to the side with concern lining her eyes. "You look a little green around the gills. Do we need to go somewhere else?"

Lucy hated to do it, but she really needed some air. "Maybe if we just step out a second. The smell of dill pickles is really getting to me for some reason."

They stepped out onto the street, where Lucy sucked in a big lungful of fresh air and felt a million times better. The queasiness was still there, but she didn't feel like she was about to make a mess in the deli during the lunch rush. "Thanks. I don't know what's gotten into me lately. I felt puny yesterday, too. I thought maybe it was the chicken sandwich I'd had for lunch, but I should be over that by now. I had a bagel and coffee for breakfast. Pickles have never bothered me before. I love pickles."

"My dad told me that when my mom was pregnant with Oliver, she couldn't abide the smell, taste or sight of pickles. I always thought that was funny, considering it's the stereotypical pregnancy thing. Oliver has always hated pickles, too. When she was pregnant with me, she couldn't get enough of them and I love pickles."

Lucy chuckled nervously at Harper's story. "Well, that's weird, but of course, I'm not pregnant."

"I'm not saying you are. It would be a funny coincidence if you were repelled by pickles, though, since it would be Oliver's baby." Harper paused for a moment, then turned and continued to eye her critically. "Lucy, are you pregnant with my brother's baby?"

Lucy lowered herself down onto a nearby bench as she mentally ran through her biological calendar. How many days had it been? It was before Alice died. She counted on her fingers and shook her head. "No," she declared at last. "I couldn't be. I mean, we used protection. I am certain that I am not pregnant."

Harper sat down on the bench beside her. "Well, what if we popped over to the drugstore and you took a pregnancy test just so we know for sure whether you need an antacid for a stomachache or a baby registry? You haven't been feeling well. I'm sure it's just the stress of everything going on, but if you take the test, then you'll know. If it's negative, then no worries, right?"

No worries? That wasn't exactly the state of mind Lucy was in at the moment. The truth was she'd lied just now. She was anything but certain. If her math was right, her period was over two weeks late. She was never late. Her uterus was made in Switzerland. With everything else going on, she hadn't even thought about it. But she *was* late. And they *had* used protection. It was just her luck that she'd fall into the three percent failure rate.

She couldn't be pregnant. Pregnant! And with Oliver's baby. How was she going to tell him? How was she going to handle all of these changes? Just as she was about to go back to college and start her life new. This was a major complication. One she simply wasn't prepared to think through on a bench in downtown New Haven.

"Come on," Harper said. She reached out for Lucy's hand and tugged her up from her chair. "We're going to the pharmacy, you're taking that test, and then we're going someplace less smelly to eat and celebrate the fact that you aren't about to give birth to my niece or nephew."

Lucy stood up and followed Harper down the block, but in her heart, she already knew the answer. Like it or not, she was going to be Oliver Drake's baby mama.

Oliver was surprised to get a message from Lucy, asking if he would meet her for dinner. He thought she'd gone away for the weekend with Harper, but apparently they'd cut their trip short. That was fine by him. He didn't want to admit it, but he didn't like not seeing her, even if it was just for a day or two. Since she left, it seemed like she was constantly on his mind and he couldn't focus on anything else.

The place she'd chosen for dinner was busy and

on the louder side. Not exactly what he would've selected for a romantic dinner for two, but he wouldn't
complain about it. Traffic wasn't the greatest, so he
arrived to the restaurant a few minutes later than
planned and Lucy was already seated at their table.

He smiled when he came around the corner and
spied her sitting there. He couldn't help it. It had
only been a few weeks and yet just the sight of
Lucy made his whole body respond. The smile on
his face, the increase in his pulse, the bizarre feeling in his stomach when she looked at him…he'd
never reacted to a woman like this before. Could it
be that this was what all the poets and musicians
wrote about?

Then she looked up at him. When her gaze met
his, he instantly knew there was something wrong.
She wasn't beaming at the sight of him the way he
was at her. He tried not to frown and take it personally. It was possible she was tired. Or maybe something had happened. He didn't know much about her
family, but perhaps an emergency had brought her
back from her trip early.

"Hello, beautiful," he said as he leaned down to
give her a soft, welcome kiss.

She smiled and kissed him back, but he could
sense some hesitation there. "Thank you for coming tonight."

"Of course," Oliver said as he unbuttoned his suit
coat and sat down. "I was surprised to hear from

you. I didn't think you were coming back until to-morrow."

Lucy nodded, her expression unusually stoic. "We decided to cut the trip short. Something... uh...came up."

Oliver stiffened in his seat. He was right. He didn't like the sound of that. "Is everything okay?"

The waiter arrived with imperfect timing to get their drink orders. Oliver was forced to drop the subject for a moment and scanned the menu. "Would you be interested in sharing a bottle of cabernet with me?"

"No, thank you. I think I'm just going to have a Perrier, please."

Oliver opted for a single glass of wine instead and the waiter disappeared. "What happened? Is it something serious?"

"Everything is okay. I'm fine. Harper is fine. Serious? I would say so. Whether or not it's good or bad news depends on how you take it. I just..." her voice trailed off for a moment.

Oliver had never seen Lucy so distraught. Not even at Aunt Alice's funeral. She seemed to be tied in knots over something. "Whatever it is, you can tell me. Let me help."

"I'm sorry, Oliver. I'm just going to have to come out and say this because I don't know how to do it any other way. I spent the whole train ride back from Connecticut trying to find a good way, and there just isn't one." She took a deep breath and let it out. "I'm pregnant."

Oliver's breath froze in his lungs and his heart stuttered in his chest with shock. He sat for a moment, not breathing, not thinking, just stunned. This wasn't possible. The restaurant was loud; maybe he just hadn't heard her correctly. He grasped at that straw in desperation. "I don't think I heard you right. Could you say it again?" He leaned in this time, praying to hear anything other than Lucy telling him she was having his child.

Lucy winced slightly and move closer to him across the table as well. "You heard me just fine, Oliver. I'm pregnant. With your baby," she added, presumably to ensure he was clear on that part of the news.

He was crystal clear on that point. She wouldn't be telling him like this otherwise. The pit of his stomach wouldn't ache with dread. No, it was obvious she was having his baby. *His baby.* He didn't even know what to say to that. Formerly stunned, his brain finally kicked into overdrive with a million thoughts running through his mind all at once. He couldn't settle on one, couldn't say a word until he'd come to terms with what she'd just said.

"I don't know what happened," Lucy continued, apparently uncomfortable with his silence. "We used protection every time. It didn't even occur to me that it was the cause of why I wasn't feeling well until Harper brought it up. I bought a pregnancy test at a drugstore and took it in the bathroom thinking it would come up negative and I could stop worrying, but it was positive. I have a doctor's appointment on Wednesday, but I don't think it will change anything. The test was pretty clear. We came back early so I could tell you right away."

He tried to listen as she spoke, but it was hard to focus on anything but the punchline. When the wheel of emotions stopped spinning in his mind, it landed on anger and betrayal, which burst out of him all at once.

"Of course you wanted to tell me right away," he said in an unmistakably bitter tone. "Who wouldn't want to inform their rich boyfriend that they got knocked up the first time they had sex? It's exciting news. Worst case scenario, you've locked down eighteen years of child support payments. If you're going to get pregnant, you might as well make sure the daddy is a millionaire, right?"

"What?" She flinched as though he'd reached out and slapped her.

This obviously wasn't the reaction she was expecting. He didn't know why. Did she think he would be excited over the prospect of the potential scammer having his child? Believe that fate had intercepted and brought them together to be one big, happy family? No. Life didn't work that way without someone like her pulling all the strings.

She'd been manipulating him from the very beginning—perhaps angling for this outcome since the day they met.

"You certainly didn't waste any time," he continued. "You must have sabotaged that first condom you handed me in the garden. Pretty bold. And to think I was relieved you had one ready to go. Of course you did. My stepmother at least married my father and moved into the penthouse before she locked him down with a child and spent all his money. I guess you're in a hurry, though."

"A hurry for what?" she asked.

"Well, I mean, the judge will rule on my aunt's will soon. This really was the best way for you to ensure that you'll get a chunk of cash from the Drake family, win or lose."

A shimmer of tears flooded Lucy's big, brown eyes. Crocodile tears, he had no doubt. "Is that what you think I've done? Do you really believe I'm capable of getting pregnant on purpose? Derailing my whole life just for money?"

"Not just money, Lucy. A shit-ton of money." The flood of angry words rushed from his mouth and he was incapable of stopping them. "I had you pegged as shady from that first day. That Pollyanna ignorance when the attorney announced you were getting everything… I knew you were playing us all. Playing my aunt. Even playing Harper, unless she's in on it for a cut. I thought that if I got to know you better, I could figure out your game, but I was wrong. You're better at this than I ever expected. I was on the verge of dropping my contest of the will, you had me so convinced. I mean, well played, Lucy. Cover all your bases."

He clapped slowly with a wide smile that probably looked more like a grimace. The bitter words were the only thing keeping him from being sick. "You've set yourself up for a win-win situation. You could walk away from this with my aunt's fortune, half of mine and then that kid will be set to inherit more from my family someday. I thought Candace was crafty and cunning going after my father, but you've got her beat, hands down. You didn't have to sleep with a lonely old man to get what you wanted."

The tears in her eyes never spilled over, but the longer he talked, the redder her face got and the tighter her jaw clenched. "Yeah," she agreed in the coldest voice he'd ever heard pass from her lips. "I just had to sleep with a lonely, bitter young man instead."

Oliver laughed at her cruel retort. "Maybe I am lonely and bitter, but I never had to screw anyone to make my way in the world."

"I thought you were a better man than this, Oliver." Lucy threw her napkin on the table and got up from her seat. "Don't point fingers at me and act so self-righteous. You may not do it now or tonight or even in a year, but one night, when you're lying alone in bed, you'll realize the mistake you've made and it will be too late." She picked up her purse and slung it over her shoulder.

"Leaving so soon?" he asked as casually as he could muster. Of course she would act upset and insulted. That was part of the charade. He wouldn't let her words get to him even if every arrow painfully struck the bull's-eye in his chest. He would keep up the facade of the bored businessman unfazed by her until she was long gone. He wouldn't give her the satisfaction of knowing she'd gotten to him.

Lucy just shook her head with sadness pulling down at the corners of her mouth. "You know, I am just as surprised by this whole situation as you are. I'm actually terrified and knowing now that I'll be doing it on my own makes it that much scarier. The difference is it's going to uproot my entire life, destroy my body and take over the next twenty years of my life, and you're just going to sit back and cut a damn check. If you don't want to be a part of your child's life, then don't bother sending money. That's an insult to me and the baby. Let's just skip the paternity test game with the attorneys and pretend we never met, okay?"

"Sounds fine. At this point, I wish we hadn't."

"Me, too. Goodbye, Oliver." Turning on her heel, Lucy barely missed a collision with the waiter as she nearly ran from the restaurant.

Oliver made a point of not watching her go. Instead, he calmly accepted his wine from the waiter and sipped it, ignoring the stares of the nearby restaurant patrons. After all that, he needed a glass of wine. Or some scotch. Anything he could get his hands on, really, to dull the pain in his chest and chase away the angry tears that were threatening to expose themselves in the restaurant.

The first large sip seemed to settle him. The blood stopped rushing in his ears and he was able to take his first deep breath since he arrived at the restaurant. That was a start. Wine couldn't undo the mess he'd just found himself in, but it would get him through this painfully uncomfortable moment.

"Sir." The waiter hovered awkwardly nearby. "Will the lady be returning?"

Oliver shook his head. "She will not."

"Very well. Will you be staying to dine with us tonight?"

He might be known for being cool under pressure, but even Oliver couldn't sit here and eat as though his world hadn't just disintegrated in his hands. "No. I think I'll finish my drink and free up the table if you'd like to run the bill."

"Yes, sir." The waiter disappeared, as visibly uncomfortable on the outside as Oliver was on the inside.

Oliver went through the motions to wrap up, finished his cabernet and stuffed his wallet back in his suit pocket. Pushing up from the table, he made his way out of the restaurant and onto the noisy street. Once there, he felt his anger start to crumble into disappointment.

Why? Why had he let himself get involved with Lucy when he knew she was just playing him, and everyone else? Instead, he'd let himself get wrapped up in her smile and her freckles. He'd lost himself in the warmth of her body and the softness of her touch. And now she was going to have his child.

His child.

Oliver sighed and forced his feet down the sidewalk toward his building. It was a long walk, and he'd normally take a taxi, but he needed the time to think. It pained him to realize that as much grief and blame as he'd heaped on his father, he'd made the same mistake. He'd fallen for a woman and let himself be used. And he'd enjoyed it. Every single second. He supposed it was karma's way of teaching him that he wasn't any smarter than his father when it came to love.

Love? He didn't dare even think that word. It wasn't love. He didn't know what to call it, but it wasn't love.

One thing he did know, however, was that if Lucy was carrying his child, Oliver would be in his or her life whether Lucy liked it or not. It wasn't about money or child support or anything else but being a good father. Oliver knew what it was like to grow up without one of his parents. Cancer had stolen his mother away, greed had taken Danny's mother from his life, but Oliver had no excuse not to be there for his child.

So whether Lucy liked it or not, he would be.

Eleven

Sitting at Alice's desk, Lucy picked up the sonogram photo again, staring at the fuzzy black-and-gray image and wondering why the Fates got so much amusement by messing with her life. This tiny photo, these blurry little blobs, no bigger than a sesame seed, were about to change her life forever.

Twins, the doctor said. Not just pregnant. Pregnant with twins. She'd laughed hysterically as she looked at the two fat little circles side by side on the monitor. It was that or cry until she ran out of tears. Fraternal twins. Because a single baby wouldn't be enough of a challenge for her to raise on her own.

The doctor was concerned by her response, not

entirely sure if she was happy or sad or freaking out. Honestly, it was a combination of all three spinning in her head so fast she could hardly keep up. It was early in the pregnancy, he'd warned. Things could change. One or both could fail. Both could last to term. Be in "wait and see" mode, he'd said. Perhaps wait until her twelve-week ultrasound to confirm the twins before announcing it to everyone.

That wouldn't be a problem. Lucy doubted she could say the words aloud. She'd hardly known what to say to him and the nurse anxiously watching her in the exam room. All she could do was lay there in her crinkly paper dress and watch her world start to crumble around her.

Putting the picture aside, Lucy focused on sorting through the apartment brochures she'd brought home from Yale. It was hard to believe how much her life had changed since she'd gotten on a train and toured that first apartment with Harper. Now, she was not just going back to college, she was doing it while pregnant. Hugely pregnant. She was having twins by herself. And even that was hard to focus on while she was also completely heartsick.

Somehow, the idea of Oliver thinking she was scamming his aunt hadn't hurt her that much. He didn't really know her, and given his past experience with his stepmother, she understood his suspicions. It was a lot of money to give someone who wasn't family. If she had been in his shoes, she might've had the same concerns, even if she didn't need a penny of Alice's money.

But when he accused her of getting pregnant on purpose—to hedge her bets, so to speak—that stung.

She wasn't just some woman he hardly knew anymore. How many hours had they spent together over the last month? How many times had they made love and held each other? Enough to know she wouldn't do something like that.

And yet there wasn't a single moment, a flicker of expression across his face at that restaurant, where the news of her pregnancy stirred anything but anger in him. He'd probably think that her having twins would be karmic retribution for her scheming.

Lucy looked down at the apartment brochure for the place she'd liked the best. The price for the two-bedroom was pretty steep. Add tuition and books, furniture, baby *everything times two*...she wasn't even certain she could afford it all. Not on what she had saved, and that was all she could count on getting. Oliver certainly wasn't going to back down on his protest of the will. The news of her "deliberately trapping" him with a pregnancy would likely hurt her case, so odds were she wouldn't see a dime of Alice's estate.

In truth, that was fine by her. That was more money than she could fathom, much less handle properly. She was much better at barely getting by.

Her mother had taught her well. But getting by with babies meant a job with medical insurance for all of them. Day care expenses times two. Diapers times two. Chaos times two. She'd always admired her mother's ability to make it work, but could she do the same?

She let the brochure fall from her fingers down to the desk as tears began to well in her eyes. Could she even do this? Was going back to school a pipe dream now? Was it smarter to put her savings into a place to live and things for the babies instead? Hell, maybe she needed to spend it on a plane ticket back home to Ohio. At least there, she would have her mother to help her with the twins. And she wouldn't run the risk of seeing Oliver again.

"Yes, this was absolutely deliberate, you ass," she said aloud to Alice's large, empty office. "I ruined all of my plans of going back to school and building my future so I could trap you with a child. Because that's the best way to keep a man you love in your life forever. But you get the last laugh, don't you? Twins!"

Lucy dropped her face into her hands and let the tears fall in earnest. She hadn't really let herself cry yet. It had been almost a week since the trip to New Haven and her breakup with Oliver, but she hadn't really let herself wallow in it. It seemed like a misuse of valuable time. Instead, she'd tried to keep herself busy with other things. After her earth-shattering doctor's appointment, she spent hours in different stores, studying everything from prenatal vitamins and stretch-panel jeans to onesies and twin strollers.

It was a tough realization to find she was completely unprepared for any of this. Before Oliver came around, she'd almost forgotten she had a uterus, much less spent time anticipating it to have not just one but two nine-month occupants. Kids were a far-off idea. One that came after love and marriage and the decision that it was time to start a family with someone she could count on.

At least she'd found the love part. Lucy did love Oliver. He didn't love or trust her one iota, but she had done her part and fallen for him. She knew now why they called it falling in love. It had been that easy, like tripping and smacking her face against the rough, hard sidewalk. Like a fall, she wasn't expecting it, but all of a sudden there she was, in love with Oliver. She could only hope that falling out of love with him was just as easy.

Easing back in the desk chair and resting her hand on her flat tummy, she knew that wouldn't be the case. Getting over him would be hard. Especially with two tiny, blue-eyed reminders of him staring at her from their cribs each morning.

It was easier than she expected to picture two wide-eyed toddlers standing in their crib in matching footie pajamas. Wild brown curls. Devious smiles. Pink cheeks. One sucking his thumb with a furrowed brow of concern while his sister clutched her favorite stuffed bunny and tried climbing over the side. In her mind, they looked like tiny clones of Oliver, although the boy had her freckles across his nose.

It was just a daydream, not a reality, but it made Lucy's heart ache. Life didn't always go to plan, but that didn't mean that she couldn't come up with a new plan. She needed to find a way to be happy about this, no matter what happened with Oliver or the will or with school. Things would work out and she had to keep that in mind. One of the pregnancy books she'd picked up had mentioned how her emotions could impact the babies. She didn't want that. No matter what happened, they would be just as loved and cared for as if they'd been planned.

A ring of the apartment's phone pulled her out of her thoughts. No one really called that line except for the doorman, so Lucy reached out and picked it up off the desk. "Hello?"

"Good morning, Miss Campbell. I have a large delivery for you."

Lucy frowned. A large delivery? She hadn't bought anything. "Are you sure it's for me? Where is it from?" she asked.

"I'm sure. It's from the Museum of Modern Art. It's another painting for the collection, ma'am."

The staff at the building was used to priceless

paintings and sculptures being delivered to Alice's apartment. Every few months, something would catch her eye on an auction website and a new piece would arrive. The difference this time being that Alice was deceased and Lucy hadn't bought any art. There had to be a mistake.

"Send them up," she said. She wouldn't know for sure until she saw what it was. Perhaps Alice had a piece on loan to MoMA that Lucy had forgotten about and was being returned.

About ten minutes later, two men came out of the freight elevator with a painting in a wooden crate. Lucy stood holding the service entrance door open as they brought it inside. "Where would you like it?" the older of the two men asked.

"The gallery," she said. That's where most of the paintings went, so it was a knee-jerk response. "I'd like to see what's inside before you leave, however. I didn't buy anything. This may be a mistake and if so, I'll want you to take it back with you."

After they set down the box, the second man pulled a sheet of paper out of his pocket. "You're Miss Lucille Campbell, right?"

"That's me," she replied, even more confused. If it was a piece on loan, it would've had Alice's name on it, not hers.

"Then this is for you."

The older man pulled out a crowbar to pry open the side and expose the painting. They carefully

pulled it out of the straw and paper bedding that
protected it and held it up for Lucy to inspect.

She remembered the painting now. It was one of
the items available at the silent auction. The painting of the New York skyline made entirely out of
hearts. She'd loved it, but she hadn't bought it.

In an instant, that whole amazing night came
flooding back to mind. Touring the museum with
Oliver, leaving early after getting overheated, making love—and conceiving the twins—on the rooftop
garden. There was only one painful answer to where
this had come from—Oliver bought it for her that
night before they left and it was just now arriving.

The timing was agonizing.

"You can leave it there," she said, indicating the
wall where it was leaning.

The men nodded, gathered up the box and pack-
ing materials and made their way back out the door.
Lucy watched them leave, then stood looking puz-
zled at the painting in front of her.

What was she supposed to do with it?

Part of her wanted to set it on fire, just to spite
him. She didn't need a reminder of that night hanging on the wall, taunting her about everything she'd
lost. But destroying it was an insult to the artist and
the painting. It didn't have anything to do with the
situation with Oliver, and she loved art too much to
consider it for long. Besides, she wasn't sure how
much he'd paid for it, but since she'd turned down

child support in her anger, she might need to sell the piece to support the twins. Unlike everything else in the apartment, that belonged only to her. His romantic gesture come too late.

The thought made her knees quiver beneath her. Better safe than sorry, she lowered herself down to the cold, marble floor of the gallery. There, she had a better view of the painting. She really did love it. Under any other circumstances, she'd be thrilled to own it. It was just a painful reminder of Oliver that she didn't need.

Staring at it for a moment, she reached out and ran her finger along the edge of the painting. Lucy knew then that she would keep it. If nothing else, it might be the only thing the twins would have from their father.

With a sigh, she stood up and went in search of a place to hang it.

Oliver was miserable.

There just wasn't any other way to describe how he felt. He wasn't even entirely sure how long it had been since he spoke with Lucy and found out about the baby. The days had all started to blur together. He hadn't been in the office. Hadn't left his apartment. He hadn't even gone up to the roof to start trimming back for the fall because being up there reminded him too much of Lucy and the night they'd spent together there. Somehow, even his sanctuary was tainted by the situation.

He wouldn't go so far as to say Lucy had ruined it. He wasn't that ignorant. It had taken a few days for his temper to cool down so he could come to that conclusion, but he knew it was true. Start to finish, this was a mess of his own making. Nothing Lucy had done since the day he met her had warranted the horrible things he'd said to her at dinner that night. She had immediately come to him to do the right thing and tell him about the baby, and he'd thrown it in her face. And yet, after hours spent racking his brain for a way to undo the things he'd done, he'd come up with nothing.

Was that even possible?

Oliver Drake: CEO and savior of Orion Technology, eligible bachelor, millionaire and complete asshat.

He was stewing on his sofa when there was a knock at the door. That in itself was unusual since the doorman hadn't called. At the same time, it was concerning. He'd dodged calls from his family for days and they were the only ones who could get up here without his permission. He hoped Harper hadn't arrived to chew him out. He hadn't even bothered to listen to the fifteen voice-mail messages she'd left him.

With a frown, he turned off the television and crossed the room to the front door. Peering through the peephole, he was relieved to find his father and brother there instead of his sister. "Dad?" he asked as he opened the door.

Tom Drake looked at his son and shook his head. "You look like hell," he said, pushing past Oliver into the house with Danny in his wake.

His little brother had recovered remarkably well from his accident. You'd hardly even know he'd been in the hospital as he took off for the living room and changed the channel to pull up his favorite show. Oliver knew that when he was bored with that, he'd whip his latest gaming device out of his back pocket and play until Dad made him stop. Technology ran deep in the veins of this family.

With a sigh, Oliver shut the door behind his dad and followed him to the kitchen where he was making himself some coffee.

"I didn't think you drank coffee anymore, Dad."

Tom looked up at him with a dismayed frown. "It's not for me, it's for you."

"I don't need any coffee, Dad. I'm not hungover."

His father narrowed his eyes at Oliver, taking in the robe and pajama pants he had on, the week-old scruff that had grown on his face and his bed-head. "Even if you're not hungover, you're drinking this," he said at last. "You need something to wake you up."

"I'm not sleepy."

"I'm not saying you are. Sometimes in a man's

life, he needs to wake up and take a look at what's going on around him. He gets too set in his ways, gets lost in a routine and doesn't notice things right in front of his face. I was like that once. I don't want you to end up like me."

Oliver scratched his head in confusion but accepted the coffee his father handed him.

"Sit down, son."

Oliver sat down at the kitchen table, trying not to think about the breakfast he'd shared here with Lucy. "I just needed a break, Dad."

Tom reached into the refrigerator and pulled out a bottle of water before sitting across from his son. "The hell you did. This is about that woman. Lucy."

Oliver hadn't said two words to his father about what had happened with Lucy, so his sister must've narc'd on him. "She's pregnant, Dad." It was the first time the words had passed his lips. Even days later, it felt alien on his tongue.

His father shrugged off his bombshell announcement. "It happens. What are you doing to do about it?"

"I don't know. I'm worried I'm going to make the same mistakes you did. I don't know that I can trust her. The whole family thinks she's some kind of crook."

"What do you think?"

"I…" Oliver stopped. He'd wrestled with this question since the day he'd met her. Now, he tried to answer honestly just as he knew her, not letting his fears answer for him. "I don't think she had anything to do with Aunt Alice changing her will. These last few weeks, I've found that Lucy is naturally charming. I think Alice would've wanted to help her out and do something nice for Lucy by leaving her the estate. At least that's my guess. But what if I'm wrong? What if she's just like Candace? How do I know the child isn't just another ploy to get her hands not only on Aunt Alice's money but mine, too?"

"You don't," his father said simply. With a sigh, Tom ran his hand through his mostly gray hair. "I think this is all my fault."

Oliver perked up in his chair. "What?"

"I thought you were old enough when all this happened with Candace, but I think I still managed to give you some trust issues. Listen, I was an idiot, Oliver. I got all wrapped up in your stepmother and made some choices that were pretty foolish in retrospect. But I was lonely so I took that chance. And now, years later, I would probably do everything exactly the same if I were given the chance to go back in time."

That surprised Oliver. He thought for sure that his father regretted what happened with his second wife. "Really?"

Tom chuckled at his son's surprise and sipped his water thoughtfully. "Yes. Despite our outward appearances, Candace and I really did have chemistry. She certainly put a dent in my finances, but it was a fine price to pay for a couple fun years and that little boy in the living room. If changing the past with Candace means that I wouldn't have Danny, then I want no part of it."

Both men turned toward the living room to watch Danny as he sat cross-legged on the floor and grinned at the television.

"Things don't always happen the way you plan, but that doesn't mean they didn't work out the way they were supposed to. If you believe Lucy didn't scheme her way into Alice's will, why would you think she's trying to trap you by getting pregnant? Maybe it was an honest mistake."

Oliver turned back to the table and studied the mug in his hands. The look on Lucy's face in the restaurant came to his mind. With a little time and perspective, he was able to see how scared she was to tell him. How hard she struggled to hide how nervous and confused she was over the pregnancy. She'd needed him in that moment and he'd failed her by turning on her and accusing her of such horrible things.

"Here's a better question," his father continued. "Does it really matter? Will it make you love your child any less?"

"No." That question was easier for Oliver to answer. If he'd figured anything out over the last few days, it was that he would love that child more than anyone on the planet had ever loved their child. The harder question was whether he was willing to love the mother just as much.

"And how did you feel about Lucy before you found out about the baby?"

"I thought that maybe I was falling in love. I guess that scared me. I've never felt that way about a woman before. It all happened so fast."

"It was that way with your mother, you know? We went from our first date to married in two months. It was intense and scary and wonderful all at once, but I couldn't stand the idea of being apart from her."

Oliver had never heard that about his parents before. He supposed that he hadn't asked, thinking it would be a sore spot for his father after his mother died. "Why did you decide to get married so quickly?"

Tom smiled and reached out to pat Oliver's shoulder. "You. Like I said before, it happens." He got up from the table and called out to Danny. "Daniel, we're getting ready to go." Then he turned back to Oliver and handed him a small box that had been stuffed into his coat pocket. "When you make up your mind, this might come in handy. It was your mother's. Talk to you later, son."

Before Oliver could really respond to everything his father had just said to him, his brother was gingerly giving him a hug and the two of them were out the door.

Alone in his apartment again, Oliver reached for the box on the table and opened the hinged lid. Inside, he found what could only be his mother's engagement ring. It was marquise-shaped with a single baguette on each side, set in platinum. It wasn't at all fashionable at the moment; it was more a throwback to another time. But it was simple, elegant and classic—the perfect ring for his mother, and he realized, perfect for Lucy as well. His mother had been one in a million and Lucy didn't fit into the mold either. It was just the ring he would choose for the mother of his child and his future wife.

If she would accept it.

In that moment, he wanted her to accept it more than he ever expected. Not just because of the baby, but because he was in love with her. Despite his suspicious nature and cautious approach, Lucy had slipped past all his defenses and reached a part of him that he'd managed to keep locked away from all the women before her. He didn't want to lock away that part of himself any longer. Like his garden, he wanted to share it with her. Share it with their child.

There was another knock at the door, startling him. Oliver got up, presuming Danny left something behind, but when he opened the door, he found a fuming Harper standing there instead. It was time to get the earful he'd avoided all week.

"You are a jerk! How could you possibly accuse Lucy of getting pregnant on purpose? That's absolutely absurd! She had plans, you know? That's why we were in Connecticut. She was planning on going back to college. How is she supposed to do that raising your baby on her own, huh? Especially with you holding all of Aunt Alice's money hostage for no good reason!"

With a sigh, Oliver stepped back to let his seething sister inside. He could tell she was just getting warmed up. Once she was done yelling at him, perhaps she could help him figure out how exactly he could clean up the mess he'd made with Lucy so everyone could be happy again.

Twelve

"Lucy, this is Phillip Glass. How are you?"

Lucy nervously clutched the phone. She hadn't heard from Alice's estate attorney in quite a while. Had the judge made a ruling yet? "Good," she answered and held her breath.

"Excellent. Well, I'm calling because I have some good news for you. Amazing news, actually. Mr. Drake has dropped his dispute over Alice's will."

Lucy slumped down into a nearby chair as her knees gave out from under her. Surely she hadn't heard him correctly. "What?"

"It's all yours now, Lucy. The money, the apartment, the art, all of it. Congratulations."

She knew she should say something, but she didn't have any words. This was not the call she was expecting to get. She'd prepared herself for the consoling discussion about how the judge felt Alice's state of mind may have been compromised at her age and given the change was so close to her death… Instead, she found she really truly had the winning lotto ticket in her hand.

An initial wave of relief washed over her. Not excitement, but relief. She'd been twisting her stomach into knots the last few days trying to figure out how she was going to support the twins on her own. Now, that question was answered and it didn't require her to go crawling to the twins' father. Although it did raise a curious question.

"Did Mr. Drake say why he dropped the protest?"

"He didn't. Honestly, I wish I knew what changed his mind, as well. Listen, I'm going to work on getting everything transitioned over to you and I'll be in touch in a week or two. There's some paperwork and hoops still to jump through, a huge chunk of estate taxes to pull out, but you can finally celebrate, Lucy."

"Thanks, Phillip."

Lucy hung up the phone and found herself still too stunned to move from her seat. She was more surprised by Oliver changing his mind than anything else. There had always been the possibility that the judge would rule in her favor, but she never thought he would back down, even when they'd gotten so close. That seemed too much like mixing business and pleasure where he was concerned.

What had changed?

Oliver had been so angry with her that night. He told her he didn't even want anything to do with his child and now, he was just handing over his aunt's estate after weeks of fighting over it? Was this his roundabout way of providing child support without paying a dime of his own money? She didn't dare to dream that it was an olive branch or first step on their way to reconciliation. Two miracles wouldn't happen in one day.

Lucy wasn't quite sure what to do. She felt like she should tell someone, and yet she was hesitant to even now. It didn't feel real. It never had. Just like looking at that sonogram.

An hour before, she'd been wondering if she could fit a bed and two cribs in the one-bedroom apartment near campus and now she could buy a house and a car, hire a full-time nanny and not have to work. Her life was undergoing a major upheaval every couple of days and she wasn't sure how many more big changes she could take.

She knew she should be excited. She was an instant millionaire hundreds of times over. Rich beyond her wildest dreams. Her children would never want for anything the way she had. Their college was paid for. Her college was paid for. Life should be easier, at least on that front. While she felt a bit of the pressure lifting from her shoulders, she still wouldn't call herself excited.

How could she be excited or happy with the way things ended with Oliver? It was impossible. All the money in the world wouldn't bring the man she loved and the father of her children back into her life. Honestly, she'd trade every penny in a heartbeat if he would knock on the door right now and tell her that he was sorry—that he loved her and their babies more than anything else. But that wouldn't happen. Not after all the horrible things he'd said. Oliver wouldn't change his mind and Lucy couldn't forget it.

The doorbell rang the moment after the thought crossed her mind, startling her from the sad path her thoughts had taken. She stood up from her seat, the phone still clutched in her hand from Phillip's call. Could it be?

Her heart started pounding in her chest, even as she tried to convince herself that it was probably the cleaning lady or Harper checking on her. Lucy stood at the door a moment, willing herself not to be disappointed if she opened it and found someone else.

Taking a deep breath, she opened it. And there, against all odds, was Oliver.

He was standing in the marble-tiled foyer looking like a tall glass of water to a woman lost in the desert. He was wearing her favorite gray suit with a blue shirt that made his eyes an even brighter shade than usual. His lips were pressed together anxiously, even as he clutched a bouquet of bright pink roses and blue delphinium in his hands.

"Hi," he said after a few long seconds of staring silently at one another.

Lucy wasn't quite sure what to think. She'd hardly recovered from the shock of her call with Phillip. "Hello." That was a start.

She took a step back to let him into the apartment. She was curious about what he had to say, but wouldn't allow herself to mentally leap ahead. Just because he was here didn't mean he was begging for her back. She didn't know what he wanted, or if she was even willing to give it to him if he did. She loved him, but she loved herself and her babies, too, and she knew she had to be smart about this. He'd been unnecessarily cruel to her and it would take more than a "sorry" and some flowers for her to forget the things he'd said.

"These are for you," he said, holding out the flowers and smiling sheepishly at her. "I picked out the pink and blue flowers for the baby."

"Thank you." Lucy accepted the flowers and turned her back on Oliver to put them in water. She needed a moment without his soulful eyes staring into her own.

When she returned from the kitchen, he was still standing in the same spot in the gallery, only now he was looking at the painting he'd bought her. She'd finally hung it on the wall.

"Thank you for the painting," she said, stopping alongside him to admire the piece. "You didn't have to do that."

"I know I didn't. That was the point of the gift."

Lucy set the vase of flowers onto the table in the entryway and turned to him. "You also didn't have to drop your contest of Alice's will. We could've seen it through to the judge and let him rule on it."

Oliver turned to her and shook his head. "No, we couldn't. I couldn't risk the judge's ruling. I dropped the suit because I changed my mind."

Lucy crossed her arms defensively over her chest. Standing this close to Oliver again after these horrible few days, she felt like she needed the buffer to protect herself. From herself.

"You changed your mind about what?" she snapped. "That I was a seasoned con artist that manipulated your elderly, agoraphobic aunt into leaving me all her money? Or that I deliberately got pregnant to trap you into financially supporting me and your child for life?"

Oliver swallowed hard, the muscles in his throat moving with strain and difficulty. She'd never seen him so tense. Not in the lawyer's office that first day, not even in the restaurant when she saw him last. He appeared outwardly calm, but she was keenly aware of how tightly strung he seemed.

"I'm sorry, Lucy," he said at last. "I'm sorry for all of that. I never should've given a voice to the doubts in my head, because that's all they were— my own demons twisting reality. You never did anything to deserve the way I treated you. You're nothing like my stepmother and I knew that, I was just afraid because I had feelings for you that I didn't know how to handle. I was scared to make a mistake like my father and instead, I made an even bigger mess by ruining the best thing I had in my life. I can only hope that one day you can see it in your heart to forgive me for that. I intend to try every day for the next fifty years until you do."

Lucy stood quietly listening to his words. They seemed painfully sincere, making her heart ache in her chest for him. But he wasn't the only one who was scared. She was scared of trusting him again too soon and having her heart trampled on. "Thank you," she said. "I know it wasn't easy for you to say all of that."

"I'll admit when I'm wrong, Lucy, and I have been in the wrong since the day we met. I wish we could start all over again, but I can't change what I've done. Can you forgive me, Lucy?" he pressed with hopeful eyes gazing into hers.

She could feel the pain and regret in every word he spoke. She'd never heard a sincerer apology. "I do forgive you for the things you said and did." She sensed that wasn't quite enough for him, but she wasn't betraying her heart too quickly.

Oliver reached out and wrapped his fingers around her hand. "Thank you. I'm so happy to hear you say that because to be honest, I'm head over heels in love with you and I thought I might never get the chance to tell you." He stopped, looking at her with an obvious question on his mind. "Do you think you might be able to love me someday?"

The warmth of his skin against hers made it hard for her to focus on his words. She could feel her body start to betray her. It longed to lean in and press against the hard muscle of his chest. She wanted to breathe in the warm scent of his cologne at his throat and feel his arms wrapped around her. She fought the urge, knowing this conversation was too important. It needed to happen and it couldn't if she started rubbing against him like a contented kitten.

She forced herself to look up at him. His eyes were pleading with her. But she had to tell the truth about how she felt.

"No," she said.

Oliver did his best not to react. He knew there was a risk in coming here—that she couldn't forgive him for how he'd treated her. He'd told himself that no matter what her answer, he would accept it, even supporting his child without being in its mother's life if that's the way Lucy wanted it. And sadly, it appeared that was how she wanted it.

"Okay," he said, dropping her hand even though it was the last thing he wanted to do.

"I can't love you *someday*, Oliver. That would mean I didn't love you now. And I do." She placed a gentle hand against his cheek and smiled warmly. "Even when I was angry and hurt, I still loved you. Of course I do."

Relief washed over him all at once and he scooped her up into his arms for a huge hug. "Oh, thank goodness!" he breathed into her ear. "I haven't blown it." Pushing back to put some distance between them again, he looked her in the eyes. "So you're telling me I haven't ruined everything for us? For our new family?"

A sheen of tears appeared in Lucy's dark brown eyes. "We're going to be a family?" she asked.

"If you'll have me." Oliver scooped her hands into his and dropped down onto his knee. He'd practiced this speech twenty times since his father had given him that ring, and in the moment, with adrenaline pumping through his veins, he couldn't remember a word of it. All he could do was speak from his heart and hope that it was romantic and wonderful enough for her to accept him.

"Lucy, I have spent the last few years of my life living under a cloud of pessimism. I never believed that a woman would love me just for who I am. I saw what happened to my father and let it color my outlook of the world. A part of me had given up on the kind of love others seemed to find. And then I met you. And you challenged me at every step. You made me question everything and I'm so thankful that you did. It forced me to realize that I was hiding from my life. And it forced me to realize that I am very much in love with you.

"Unfortunately," he continued with a sheepish grin, "I didn't know how much I loved you until I'd nearly ruined everything for us. It was there, alone and miserable in my apartment, that I decided that I was willing to do anything to make it up to you, if I even could. First, I had my lawyer withdraw the protest because I wanted you to know that I believed you. Aunt Alice wanted you to have that money, and I want you to have it, too, whether or not you wanted me in your life again. There's no strings attached."

"You really, truly believe me? You have no reservations at all about the will or the baby?"

He'd failed to answer this question properly the first time because he was plagued with doubts even as she lay in his arms. Now, he was confident in his decision. "You don't have a malicious bone in your body, Lucy. I can't believe I ever thought otherwise. And if I did, I wouldn't have taken this to the jeweler to be cleaned and sized just for you."

Oliver reached into his pocket and pulled out the jewelry box his father had brought him a few days before. He opened the lid to show her the ring inside. "This ring belonged to my mother," he said as she gasped audibly. "My father gave it to me in the hopes that I would stop moping around my place and start living my life with you in it. And not just you, but with our child, too."

Lucy looked at the ring expectantly, but she didn't say anything. At first, he thought that maybe she was just dazzled by the sight of it, but Oliver quickly realized that he was so nervous, he forgot to ask the critical question.

"Lucille Campbell, will you please do me the honor of being my wife, accepting all the love I have to give and standing by my side for the rest of our lives?"

At that, Lucy smiled through her tears. "Yes," she said. "There's nothing more I want than to be your lover and partner in life."

Oliver's hands were shaking as he pulled the ring from its velvet bed and slipped it onto her finger. "It's a little large on you right now, but the jeweler suggested sizing up so you could wear it well into your second and third trimesters."

"It's perfect," she said as she admired it on her hand. "I'm honored to wear the ring your mother once wore. I know she was important to you."

He clutched her hands in his as he stood up. With his eyes pinned on hers, he leaned in and planted a kiss on the ridge of her knuckles—one hand, then the other—before seeking out her lips. When his mouth pressed to hers, it was like a promise was made between them. The engagement was official—sealed with a kiss.

He wrapped his arms around her and pulled her close. Oliver didn't want to let go. Not after almost losing her for good. She felt so right here, how could he ever have said or done something to drive her away? He was a fool once, but never again. She would be his—and he, hers—forever.

When their lips finally parted, he leaned his forehead against hers. "I want us to be a real family. Like my parents had. These last few days thinking about you raising our child without me... I couldn't bear the thought of it despite what I said that night at the restaurant. I was upset and confused about the news. It may not have been planned, but this child will always know that he or she was wanted. I'll do everything in my power to see to that. But most of all I want to make you happy, Lucy. Anything you want, we can make it happen."

"I don't know what I could possibly ask for, Oliver. Today alone, you've proposed with your mother's engagement ring and given me a half a billion dollar estate. It seems greedy to ask for anything else."

"Harper told me that you were trying to go back to school. You never mentioned it to me before."

"Yes," Lucy hesitated. "That was my plan, but..."

"No buts. If you want to go back to Yale, you absolutely should do it."

"It's so far away, Oliver. From you and your job. I don't want to be alone in Connecticut while you're here running your computer company."

Oliver just shrugged off her concerns. "If you want to be in Manhattan every night, I'll have you flown to class and back on Orion's private jet each day. If you want to stay there during the week, we'll buy a nice place and I'll come spend every weekend I can with you until you graduate."

"I don't know," Lucy said. "That seems like it would make things far more complicated than they need to be. If I was moving up there by myself as I'd planned originally, that's one thing, but I'm not leaving you behind. Maybe I can look at some of the local programs. I'm sure Columbia or NYU has something that will allow me to stay in the city. And when the babies—er, *baby*—comes," she stuttered, "we'll all be together. That's the most important thing."

Oliver grinned. Of course, he preferred having her as close as possible, but that was completely up to her. "Are you sure? Like I said, whatever makes you happy, Lucy."

"Being with you makes me happy." Leaning in, she rested her head on his shoulder and sighed in contentment. "After everything that has happened, I may even defer school for another year or two.

I'm not sure I can manage a wedding, a pregnancy and caring for an infant on top of the senior-level classes I need to graduate. The art will always be there when I'm ready. I want to focus on remembering every moment of these early months with you."

"If that's what you want." Oliver smiled. They certainly did have a lot coming up in their lives over the next year. "And don't forget, we have to decide where we want to live. We have two amazing Manhattan apartments to choose from."

"I want to move to your place," Lucy said without hesitation. "For one thing, I couldn't ask you to leave your beautiful garden. And for another, Alice's place is stunning, but way too formal and stuffy for children running around all wild."

Oliver smiled at her decision. "Children, huh? Are we already planning on having more than one?"

A curious expression came across Lucy's face. She wrinkled her nose and bit at her lip. "There's something I need to tell you," Lucy admitted.

"Yes? Anything, love."

"The doctor says we're having twins."

Twins? The room began to spin and close in on him.

Oliver was about to experience a lot of new firsts. His first time in love, his first time to be engaged, his first children were on the way... And this was the first time he'd ever fainted.

He was out cold before he hit the floor.

Epilogue

Lucy eyeballed the three paint swatches on the walls of what would soon be the twins' nursery. Three months later, they were both growing and thriving, pressing Lucy's belly out to a larger bulge than she anticipated this far along. She and Oliver had decided not to find out the sex of the twins, so she was comparing different shades of gray paints for the neutral design they had planned.

With her hands planted on her hips, she frowned at the wall and continued to after Oliver came up behind her. "The one in the middle," he said without hesitation. "And Emma is on the phone for you."

Emma's baby girl, Georgette, had been born right

after Lucy announced her pregnancy. Little Georgie, named after her maternal grandfather, George Dempsey, had occupied most of Emma's time the last three months. Lucy accepted the phone from Oliver, curious as to what prompted the call from her friend.

"Hey, Emma," Lucy said. "I'm trying to pick out a color for the nursery. What's going on with you?"

"It's not me I'm calling about, it's Violet."

Lucy didn't like the way her friend said that. "What's wrong? Are she and the baby okay?" Violet was due any day now.

"They're both fine. She delivered a healthy baby boy this morning."

"That's wonderful!" Lucy gushed. "I'm glad you called, I hadn't heard anything yet. Stupid Beau. He was supposed to let us know when she went into labor."

"Yeah, well…" Emma said. "There's a reason he didn't call."

The feeling of anxiety returned to Lucy's stomach. "What's that?"

"It turns out the baby isn't his."

Lucy's jaw dropped. "What? How do they know that? Did he demand a paternity test so soon after she delivered?"

"No," Emma replied. "They didn't need one. Beau and Violet are both dark haired, dark skinned and dark eyed. Mediterranean lineage through and through."

"And the baby?"

"The baby is a fair-skinned, blue-eyed redhead."

A redhead? Violet had never once mentioned anything about a dating a ginger. She'd been on again, off again with Beau for the last few years, but even then, Violet hadn't dated anyone else. At least that Lucy knew about. "Then who *is* the father?"

"That's just it. No one knows. Not even Violet. Apparently she conceived the baby just before her car accident. When she hit her head and got amnesia, she lost the whole week, including any memories of being with someone else. She doesn't remember who her baby's father is!"

* * * * *

COMING NEXT MONTH FROM

HARLEQUIN® *Desire*

Available March 6, 2018

#2575 MARRIED FOR HIS HEIR
Billionaires and Babies • by Sara Orwig
Reclusive rancher Nick is shocked to learn he's a father to an orphaned baby girl! Teacher Talia loves the baby as her own. So Nick proposes they marry for the baby—with no hearts involved. But he's about to learn a lesson about love...

#2576 A CONVENIENT TEXAS WEDDING
Texas Cattleman's Club: The Impostor
by Sheri WhiteFeather
A Texas millionaire must change his playboy image or lose everything he's worked for. An innocent Irish miss needs a green card immediately after her ex's betrayal. The rule for their marriage of convenience: don't fall in love. For these two opposites, rules are made to be broken...

#2577 THE DOUBLE DEAL
Alaskan Oil Barons • by Catherine Mann
Wild child Naomi Steele chose to get pregnant with twins, and she'll do anything to earn a stake for them in her family's oil business. Even if that means confronting an isolated scientist in a blizzard. But the man is sexier than sin and the snowstorm is moving in... Dare she mix business with pleasure?

#2578 LONE STAR LOVERS
Dallas Billionaires Club • by Jessica Lemmon
PR consultant Penelope Brand vowed to never, ever get involved with a client again. But then her latest client turns out to be her irresistible one-night stand, and he introduces her as his fiancée. Now she's playing couple, giving in to temptation...and expecting the billionaire's baby.

#2579 TAMING THE BILLIONAIRE BEAST
Savannah Sisters • by Dani Wade
When she arrives on a remote Southern island to become temporary housekeeper at a legendary mansion, Willow Harden finds a beastly billionaire boss in reclusive Tate Kingston. But he's also the most tempting man she's ever met. Will she fall prey to his seduction...or to the curse of Sabatini House?

#2580 SAVANNAH'S SECRETS
The Bourbon Brothers • by Reese Ryan
Savannah Carlisle infiltrated a Tennessee bourbon empire for revenge, *not* to fall for the seductive heir of it all. But as the potential for scandal builds and one *little* secret exposes everything, will it cost her the love of a man she was raised to hate?

YOU CAN FIND MORE INFORMATION ON UPCOMING HARLEQUIN® TITLES, FREE EXCERPTS AND MORE AT WWW.HARLEQUIN.COM.

HDCNM0218

Get 2 Free Books,
Plus 2 Free Gifts—
just for trying the Reader Service!

HARLEQUIN *Desire*

"You'll get to meet my brother tonight."

Penelope was embarrassed she didn't know a thing about
another Ferguson sibling. She'd only been in Texas for a
year, and between juggling her new business, moving into
her apartment and handling crises for the Dallas elite, she
hadn't climbed the Ferguson family tree any higher than
Chase and Stefanie.

"Perfect timing," Chase said, his eyes going over her
shoulder to welcome a new arrival.

"Hey, hey, big brother."

Now, that…that was a drawl.

The back of her neck prickled. She recognized the voice
instantly. It sent warmth pooling in her belly and lower. It
stood her nipples on end. The Texas accent over her shoulder
was a tad thicker than Chase's, but not as lazy as it'd been

two weeks ago. Not like it was when she'd invited him home and he'd leaned close, his lips brushing the shell of her ear.

Lead the way, gorgeous.

Squaring her shoulders, Pen prayed Zach had the shortest memory ever, and turned to make his acquaintance.

Correction: reacquaintance.

She was floored by broad shoulders outlined by a sharp black tux, longish dark blond hair smoothed away from his handsome face and the greenest eyes she'd ever seen. Zach had been gorgeous the first time she'd laid eyes on him, but his current look suited the air of control and power swirling around him.

A primal, hidden part of her wanted to lean into his solid form and rest in his capable, strong arms again. As tempting as reaching out to him was, she wouldn't. She'd had her night with him. She was in the process of assembling a firm bedrock for her fragile, rebuilt business and she refused to let her world fall apart because of a sexy man with a dimple.

A dimple that was notably missing since he was gaping at her with shock. His poker face needed work.

"I'll be damned," Zach muttered. "I didn't expect to see you here."

"That makes two of us," Pen said, and then she polished off half her champagne in one long drink.

Don't miss
LONE STAR LOVERS
by Jessica Lemmon, the first book in the
***DALLAS BILLIONAIRES CLUB** trilogy!*

Available March 2018 wherever
Harlequin® Desire books and ebooks are sold.

www.Harlequin.com

Want to give in to temptation with
steamy tales of irresistible desire?

Check out **Harlequin® Presents®,
Harlequin® Desire** and
Harlequin® Kimani™ Romance books!

New books available every month!

LOVE
Harlequin
romance?

Join our Harlequin community to share your thoughts and connect with other romance readers!

Be the first to find out about promotions, news, and exclusive content!

Sign up for the Harlequin e-newsletter and download a free book from any series at

www.TryHarlequin.com

CONNECT WITH US AT:

Harlequin.com/Community

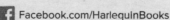 Facebook.com/HarlequinBooks

 Twitter.com/HarlequinBooks

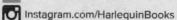 Instagram.com/HarlequinBooks

 Pinterest.com/HarlequinBooks

ReaderService.com

**ROMANCE WHEN
YOU NEED IT**